1

ESCAPE

*T*HE CAVALRY OFFICER *lives and dies by the open field.*
This day, death rides on my heels.

My horse's hooves hammered over stone, and my thundering heart echoed their panicked rhythm. As we raced through a desolate wasteland, the *whoosh* of wind roared a duet with the throb of my pulse in my ears. It galled me to flee my enemies. But all other options had drained away with the blood of my dwindling squadron.

Get out of the open.

I pounded my heels into Solaris's flanks, and he redoubled his efforts at haste. A second horse galloped behind me, but the diminished volume of his footfalls told me I outpaced him. I glanced back. Indeed, Captain Curunith gripped his reins and tugged his horse's mouth where he should have been giving the beast his head to better navigate the terrain. Although our service together had drawn us closer than brothers, that familiarity had failed to imbue him with any of my horsemanship. Curunith rode farther behind me than the last time I had checked. I slowed to a stop, sparing a moment to pat my mount's sweat-lathered neck.

"Rest will come soon, friend." I winced. Solaris had earned better than my lies.

While he closed the distance between us, Curunith fished in his saddlebag. He slowed his horse, just as I was about to spur mine into motion again. *No time*, my spinning thoughts raged.

"Vinyanel, wait." Curunith extended a black chalice to me. "We need to adjust our withdrawal strategy."

"Put that cursed thing away, Captain," I said. "We need to strategize on the move."

"You must take it," Curunith said. "I will lead as many of the dragon-kin as I can on a false trail, into the eastern grasslands. Solaris will bear you beyond harm if he can lend you his full speed, without my poor riding to slow you."

I clasped the chalice. Some foul warlock had cast it from the black blood of a demon and ringed the lip of the vessel with basilisk teeth. A shudder ran through my arm, as though the thing slipped slimy tentacles over my flesh when I touched it.

My sole surviving companion on this mission—dare I forsake his company? If our enemies did catch up to me, I could not deny the truth that the fewer, the better.

Curunith wheeled his horse to the east. "Creo speed you, brother-in-arms. I will see you at Delsinon's gates." His frail smile and the flatness in his eyes betrayed his confident words. We locked glances for a fraction of a moment in silent farewell. He maneuvered onto a twisted path that meandered into the inhospitable wastes and picked up a canter without looking back.

I jammed the chalice into my pack, unconcerned for its care, and yet biting down hard on a swell of emotion. I had no time for frailty. The weight of the mission now bore down on me alone.

Vindicate our losses.

With one last glance over my shoulder, I caught a glimpse of Captain Curunith as he slipped into the concealing embrace of the rocks and heather. He left a clear churn of hoof prints in the sandy soil. But would his false trail be the help we hoped, or just speed both our deaths?

For that moment, I was alone—utterly alone. At least that left me in command of no others. I risked only my own flesh now. Beads of sweat snaked down my face, renewing the sting of claw gouges on my cheekbones.

Solaris and I charged onward. My pack thumped against my back, its weight awkward and uneven with the drag of its new contents. How could something as insignificant as a chalice be worth all the suffering and loss we had already confronted that day? I forced the thought behind steel walls in the back of my mind. The mission commandeered every measure of my attention. Nothing mattered more than the return of the black chalice to my superiors in the Elven capitol of Delsinon—not even the shattered bond of long friendship.

The chalice, the cursed thing! While little bigger than a mundane cup, it was weightier than it looked, if the pack of dragon-kin pursuing me were any indication. Behind me, beyond the gorse-covered rises, and for now, beyond hearing, I assumed the reptilian regiment still followed. At least I had the benefit of daylight to sicken and slow them. While I still drew breath, no foul servant of the Darkness would use the cup to summon fiendish allies into the world of elves and men. The dragon-kin were formidable enough foes without the ghastly apparitions of hell to swell their ranks.

I spurred Solaris harder toward the jagged arm of the mountains that lay ahead. We wove through narrows between jutting crags of rock, and leapt the clefts where streams churned their way to lower ground. Left behind was the open dale between the mountains and the dragon-kin stronghold where I had last spied my pursuers. The thundering of Solaris's hooves grew sharper with the metallic grate and ring of his shoes on stone. Through it all, he never slackened, sensing the dire nature of our mission—

perhaps more than I. Could he smell the acrid scent of dragon-kin on the wind?

We careened along a narrow path that snaked between two shoulders of salt-white rock. Solaris's scream shattered the air. He dropped from beneath me. I flew from his back and landed hard with a rattle of plate mail and armaments.

I rolled over to find my horse lying on the ground. His flanks heaved, which I expected from his long exertion, but something about the uneven rhythm of his short breaths gripped my chest. His wild eyes and flaring nostrils cried to me in the nonverbal way we had come to understand one another over the years—my faithful mount fought great pain. I scanned his chest, barrel, hindquarters. No arrow or other attack had pierced him, so why had he fallen?

When at last I discovered the source of his distress, my stomach lurched. Six paces behind him, I found the lower half of his foreleg wedged between two close stones. Blood, bone—these had little power to trouble me; decades of battle had numbed me to such gore. But the inevitable loss of a stalwart companion slammed into me and knocked me reeling.

My head spun. *Maker's mercy, not this. There must be some way...*

I knew better. There was no time, even if there had been a glimmer of hope. In Solaris's final effort to serve me, he had seen his leg shorn off by terrain I had no business asking him to take at a gallop.

I cupped the velvet of his muzzle in my hand one lingering moment, then drew my crossbow.

Flashes of every battle, every training exercise, every time Solaris proved himself more a soldier than many who went on two legs, raced through my mind. With sluggish reticence, I fitted a bolt to the nock. The weapon uttered the groan held captive in my soul as I cocked it.

I only hoped a bolt to the forehead would end Solaris's long duty to me with dignity. I aimed the weapon.

He dropped his head to the ground and huffed an equine sigh. Though my hands shook, I lacked options. I squeezed the release. With searing finality, Solaris's last shrill cry rent my heart.

The unmistakable tramp of feet and the guttural shouts of my enemies bounced from the stone around me, garbled, but too close. I hesitated over Solaris's still body. To leave his remains for the sport of crows—or enemies—filled me with rancor. But my pursuers neared.

"Sorry, old friend," I whispered. I brushed his forelock from his unseeing eye and swallowed hard. Nausea heated my stomach and clawed at my tongue. Hefting my pack again, I rose and dashed deeper into the mountains.

M y many gashes from the morning's fight for the chalice throbbed as I pressed onward, and I searched my mind for tactical options. Could I stand my ground? Doubtful. Outrun them? The growing clamor of pursuit testified this strategy had already failed me. As a captain of the Elven cavalry, I bristled at the idea, but seeking some hiding place loomed as my only remaining option.

The path ahead of me split into an uphill road that climbed to the top of a ridge, and a lower way, choked and overhung, that hugged the rising cliff. I chose the rougher way, since it would at least force my pursuers to march single file.

I picked along the path, painfully aware that the scraggly flora clinging to the rocks offered no real cover. Sheer drops and channels that ended too soon forbade passage to my left. Then finally, a deep shadow behind a curtain of tangled growth caught my notice—dare I hope for a cave? I parted the brambles and vines that hung over the entrance. My gaze probed the darkness beyond.

As my gift of elvensight turned the interior darkness to day, I slipped my longsword from the scabbard on my hip and slunk inside the cavern. The first chamber of the cave delved about twenty paces into the mountain. The rocky floor left the footing treacherous at best, and the converging walls threatened to impede sword strokes in all but the entrance. *Too small to hide me for long. This niche had better prove more useful than a corner to cower against.* I glanced back. No enemy loomed in the entry yet.

I pressed toward the deeper recesses of the chamber and found the rear of the cave narrowed to a slim corridor. It was about time I encountered a mercy amidst the day's trials. I trod softly as a cat on the prowl. At times, the passage forced me to sidestep my way through, the fit barely accommodating the depth of my breastplate. Oddly, instead of the cave growing darker, a faint, bluish glow flickered in the distance ahead. I halted.

What devilry had I walked into? Was I forestalling one slaughter to exchange it for another? I stood frozen in the channel, and each breath, like each heartbeat, came quicker than the last. I weighed my options. To turn back to the known battle behind me, or to risk danger untested ahead? I set my jaw and forged onward. The blue light grew with every step I took.

After I spent an age scuffling and squeezing, the corridor opened into a circular, hewn chamber. Ancient runes ran in a line around the room, carven like a border. Glowing stones poked from the walls, set at intervals among the runes, bathing the cavern in unearthly hues. *Lumienne?* Out here between the wilderness and nowhere? I blinked while my eyes reverted to lightvision.

"You have been much delayed, Vinyanel Ecleriast. Surely your commanders despair of your return."

I sucked a sharp breath through my teeth. What had I missed

in my eyesight's transition? My sword flew to middle guard. I scoured the cavern with renewed acuity.

A willowy, raven-haired maiden rose from behind a stone slab that served as a sort of table. A faint tinkling drifted through the air, as her motion awoke hundreds of tiny bells that adorned her slim corset, her many-layered skirt, and the riot of scarves cascading from her body. Her fluttering, jingling softness stood in jarring contrast to that rough and unforgiving hole.

I spoke low, yet my voice resonated through the room. "How do you know my name?"

"I know all things the Creator reveals to me." She glided towards me. Only the occasional peek of a bare foot from beneath her hem told me she walked rather than floated. Though I could guess little about this strange woman, at least she was mortal. Even so, I kept my sword at mid-guard and backed in an arched path to position myself in the center of the room. My gaze remained fixed on the maiden.

As she drew near, I narrowed my eyes. *A half-elf*. Her soft-edged features and lightly pointed ears bespoke her mixed parentage. I gripped my sword until my knuckles whitened; such outcasts often earned checkered reputations.

Her penetrating amber eyes locked onto my own. "You are less than you are meant to be."

"Who are you?" I asked. "What do you want from me?"

She giggled. Actually giggled. "From you? Better to ask, what do you stand to gain from me?"

"You talk in riddles." This was no time for bandying useless words. "Unless you offer a way to evade the dragon-kin who dog my steps, I bid you leave me to my flight."

"Ah, flight, yes." She nodded, her lips twisting into a knowing curl. "You are much troubled by such a little thing."

Her aloof demeanor grated against my battle-raw nerves. "A fine conclusion for you who, I daresay, has not lost stalwart companions to the swords of enemies this day."

She sighed, the sound gently musical as she cast her gaze to the earthen floor of the cavern. "The clamor of your youth in your ears prevents you from hearing truth, young Windrider."

The brashness of her words destroyed any melody in her voice. *Young?* Her human parentage had robbed her of half the years she might have lived, and yet she called me *young*. I slammed my sword into its sheath. "Windrider? Another riddle. Explain, or do not add to my list of troubles today."

The maiden took on a distant look, as though her gaze probed into places unseen by mortal eyes. She drifted back to the stone slab, her strides controlled and dance-like. A tome bound in flaking leather lay on the slab's chiseled top. As she turned a page, the vellum crackled, its brittle sound echoing through the room. She did not look down at the book, but rested her palm over the illuminated script within. She closed her eyes, her ebony lashes a dark splash against caramel cheeks.

"On the wings of the dragon I shall bear them up. They shall soar to victory, proclaiming my glory, enacting my justice, in humbleness and mercy."

I knew the passage—but why speak it now?

"In their partnership . . ." she continued, forth-telling the message *"...they shall trumpet the loving-kindness of their Maker, as well as the dread power of my fury upon those who profane me."* The words flowed from her lips, not in an absent way, but as though they formed of their own accord.

So, she's a prophetess of some ilk, then. As the words worked their way into my soul, the wound steel of my muscles uncoiled, but caution still reigned in my soldiering mind. "I fail to see how these words clarify anything. But there is no time to unravel them. My presence puts you in danger here."

She smiled and opened her eyes, her expression growing *present* again. "I am in danger? Perhaps. But more urgent, the chalice must arrive in Delsinon. Yet you may not, with your horse slain and your enemies upon the doorstep."

What in Creo's dominion was going on here? Why would a prophetess linger in this strange wilderness?

As if to punctuate her words, the clamor of rasping voices and clanking metal echoed in the distance. I had delayed. Now I was trapped.

"You do not strike me as one prepared to stand your ground against armed foes," I said. "Tell me this cavern has another outlet, aside from the way I came."

"Follow me." The half-elf maiden sprang to me, took my hand, and towed me across the chamber, straight toward the wall. The stone ahead had neither crevice nor gap.

Perfect. Enigmatic and *daft.* I resisted her direction. Just when I thought she would recoil from the hard smack of her head upon the stone, she raked her hand across the wall. A band of opalescent glimmer appeared in the wake of her gesture. The half-elf thrust her arm into the uncanny surface and drew it out again.

"See, still whole." She held up her hand for my inspection.

I inched forward, all the while keeping an ear tuned to the groaning and tramp of pursuit. I reached for the altered section of the wall, and indeed, my hand slipped into it.

"Which will it be, skeptical warrior?"

I quirked a brow. "Very well. Lead on."

When the maiden's body touched the stone, a slash of light wrapped around her shape until she disappeared beyond it. My heart thundered. My fortune of late left it equally possible I would find a trap beyond that wall as I would an escape. Still, I drew a breath and stepped forward.

I stepped into the shimmering stone as easily as one slips through a curtain of water. A sizzling rush ran over my skin, and I shuddered down to my core. The sensation, while uncanny, had an exhilarating surge to it.

We emerged into an antechamber, and I turned to face the way we had come. The wall's gleam diminished, and the nebulous mist we had marched through reformed into apparent stone once again. I touched the wall. Solid. Daylight lanced into this chamber from somewhere above, and I tipped my chin to seek its source. I found a wide opening at the apex of this new cave, where blue sky and clouds filled the space. But that outlet was some ten stories up the wall. Without climbing gear, we had simply put one battlefield behind us to exchange for another, one where we would more clearly perceive our doom befalling us.

I wheeled back to the maiden and staggered back, whipping my weapon from its scabbard again and nearly losing my grip on the hilt in my haste. Beyond her, where the cavern fell into shadow, loomed the shape of the most enormous beast I had ever seen. My heart leapt into my throat.

The creature uncoiled from a dark antechamber with serpentine grace. His scales were like thousands of polished mirrors. His maw, instant death. But his eyes, gentle as the new leaves whose color they bore.

Once the full forty feet of his length had emerged into the light, he turned his gaze to me.

"Greetings, Vinyanel," the dragon rumbled.

I snapped my glance to the maiden. Her easy posture spoke no sense of alarm at the wyrm's arrival.

He continued. "I understand we have a delivery to make, with no time to waste."

"How is it word of what was to be a secret mission of scouting has reached two total strangers?" I blustered.

Muffled shouts rose in the indeterminable distance.

"That sounds like the least of your problems at present," the dragon said. "Let us leave behind the little mockers who so poorly reflect my kind." A shudder ran through the floor, and a sharp, stony *crack* cut through the air, intermingled with guttural words. My pursuers bellowed in a rhythmic chant.

"Quickly!" the prophetess cried.

Red arteries of light splayed across the cavern wall I had just passed through. The ground trembled. The cracks exploded with blinding light, and the wall fell away in a shower of rubble and dust. At least a dozen black hooded dragon-kin stood in the gap. They hesitated, deep cowls obscuring their reaction to the scene before them. I could guess at their thoughts.

So here it would end. I pointed my longsword at the squadron of enemies and pulled my kite shield from my back.

"Good heavens, you are a thick one!" The prophetess grabbed me by the collar of my breastplate and hauled me backward.

In the next moment, my feet lifted from the ground, and I let out a less-than-dignified yelp. I bobbled astride the dragon's snout. He arched his neck around and plunked me onto his back.

Surreal. There was no other description for the moment.

He deposited the prophetess behind me.

With a single thrust of legs and wings, our mount launched us into the air.

"A curse will follow you wherever you take what is ours!" one of the dragon-kin bellowed after us.

We sped toward the mouth of the cavern and exchanged the muted light of the chamber for the full glare of the sun. On our way through the cavern outlet, our dragon rescuer slashed his tail across the snowy peak of the mountain, and a thunderous cascade of rocks and snow tumbled into the cavern upon our foes.

The words the prophetess had read before echoed in my mind. I had always taken such passages from Creo's book of wisdom as words of beauty. Poetry, meant to be interpreted as symbolism alone. Could the Maker have some destiny of mine intertwined with the will of this daunting creature who bore me? Justice. Mercy. It all swirled through my thoughts, pregnant with meaning but beyond my comprehension.

But what of the dragon-kin's declaration of cursing? A bitter smirk tugged at my lip. Had I not already seen every woe but my own demise?

Mighty beats of the dragon's wings carried us skyward, higher with each thrust, and my ruminations dissolved in the face of sheer wonder. I clutched the dragon's dorsal plate in front of me. The ripple of his muscles, the palpable power of his breath drawing into his lungs—never had I encountered such majesty. Tears sprang to my eyes.

My every jubilant dream became reality. Lancing into the azure sky, we wheeled to the south, and the throaty protests of my enemies faded beyond hearing or care. Not even my grief kept pace with me now.

It had been a day of flight, first in retreat, and now through the boundless expanse of the heavens. Was it my destiny to glorify my Maker from the back of a dragon? In this, he would hear no protest from me. For now, I prayed the astounding majesty of flight would carry on without end.

2

THE FACETS OF MIGHT

As THE DISTANT mountains slowly slipped away beneath me, I sat slack-jawed at the matchless serenity of flight. Or it *might* have been serene, were it not for the intermittent caterwauling of the barnacle fastened to the backplate of my armor. The prophetess who rode double behind me clung to my torso with an ever-tightening grip, and each time our silver dragon mount banked or dove, she squeezed even harder and let out a keening wail that rivaled the cries of a banshee.

I claimed no immunity to the gentle wiles of a maiden's touch, yet nothing in the way this prophetess gripped me stirred the least sensation of tenderness or thrill. Her enigmatic, lofty demeanor when we met just a few short hours before had irked me to the limit of my patience, and her persistent miauling in my ear rendered powerless any subtle allure her closeness might have stirred in other circumstances. We could not arrive in the capital city soon enough for my taste. Only then would I be free of the chalice. Free of her.

"How much longer to Delsinon, friend dragon?" I called above the rushing wind and the beating rhythm of the creature's wings.

"Perhaps another three hours," the dragon called back.

Amazing. A trip that would have taken days on horseback, reduced to a mere eight hours. This dragon-riding had its advantages.

"Three hours?" the half-elven maiden whined. "Is it really so long?"

"I could fly faster and try to cut down on the time," the dragon replied.

A dark smile curved my lip.

"No!" she blurted. "Your current pace shall suffice."

Pity.

"But when we near the place, will you guide me?" the dragon asked.

I tilted my head, but a passing moment brought comprehension. He might be able to set a general course for the region where Delsinon sat shrouded behind a veil of illusion, but without a talisman of passage, even a dragon would be subject to missing what passed right beneath him. This wyrm knew of my mission to the dragon-kin stronghold—no doubt he would have earned a place as a welcome visitor to Delsinon. Frankly, he had a better chance at a friendly reception than the prophetess.

We careened on, over dense forest and rolling plain, past rivers and through misty banks of cloud from which we emerged damp and chilled. We left the mountains far behind until they vanished over the horizon, and all that remained was the verdant canopy of my homeland.

"We exchanged no introductions when we met," I said. "Both of you clearly know who I am. What shall I call you?"

"My name among elves is Majestrin," the dragon offered.

Fitting.

"You may call me—" The prophetess's words broke off in another squeal as an updraft buffeted us higher. She buried her head in my cloak. "Veranna. My name is Veranna."

I tightened my lips. So the half-elf had been given an elven name, or else adopted one at some point. Interesting, but not telling.

As the sun sank toward the horizon, I recognized beneath us telltale landmarks that assured me we drew nigh to Delsinon: the forking of the river Nuruhain that gave birth to the smaller, swifter Arin, along with the ever-thickening tangle of forest canopy, shaggy with moss tendrils and creeper. Soon, I alone would see the graceful spires of my ancient home rising from the forest. It fell to my direction to bring us to the gates.

Though I looked only briefly over my shoulder, my glance caught upon Veranna's. The quirk of her brow suggested she read something vaguely amusing in my expression, and I was in little mood to be goaded. I snapped my gaze frontward again. I slipped a talisman on a silver chain from beneath my armor and gripped it.

"A few more leagues, and you will have delivered me to the end of this crucial leg of my quest," I told Majestrin. "Will you accompany me to the door of the king's palace and receive your due accolades?"

"No, Captain Ecleriast. With the long generation that has passed since your kind and mine have shared civil discourse, I think it best you approach your city on foot. I will not be far, and you shall find me again."

"After all, this fits Creo's purpose," the prophetess added.

Does it? Was this knowledge, or did she speak from a perpetual desire to appear of loftier make than the flesh-and-blood inhabitants of Argent? *The turn of today's events still baffles me. My return home had best offer some depth of understanding of what the Maker might want of me in this "Windrider" arrangement.*

"Majestrin, do you see that sycamore to the northwest—the bare, white tree amidst the maples?" I said.

Majestrin bobbed his head.

"Circle it, counter-clockwise, then make a descent. Have a

care not to clear the maple grove before you land, or else you will lose your way entirely and we will have to start again."

We made the wide circle, and to my eyes alone, Delsinon's white fortress towers, stout wall, and graceful rooftops shimmered into view to the inside of our flight path. Despite Majestrin's careful maneuvering during our descent, branches of the dense old-growth forest still slapped at us as we passed through the canopy. The plates of my dented armor spared me the bulk of the assault. I pulled a bundle of leaves from beneath my spaulder and winced at the ugly rent in the piece.

As the dragon's fearsome talons touched the ground, his claws dug into the forest floor. The rich aroma of turned earth filled my nostrils. I breathed deeply; it was good to be home. And yet, a faint bitterness of bruised leaf came with the draught, for I also returned to Delsinon to report of those who would never breathe such scents again.

I alighted from the towering creature's back, though with a grunt when a slash wound to my ribs protested anew at the motion. With my arm opposite the pain, I raised an offer of assistance to Veranna. Whether I cared for her or not, decorum dictated I aid her in dismounting from the dragon's tall back. She slipped to the earth, her trembling hands merely an echo of the tremors that afflicted all her weary muscles. To her credit, I did not have to rescue her from buckling knees.

With her feet now firmly on the ground, she straightened. She tipped her chin higher and regarded me with eyelids half-lowered. "Shall we set out for the gate?"

My jaw slackened. "We? You mean—you and me?"

"Of course. Majestrin already said he would not come."

"Well," I blustered, "it may be unwise for you to come along. Relations between your kind and mine have often been more strained than the associations between elves and dragons."

"Nonsense. The Creator wills that I should accompany you."

I huffed. "What argument can a mere soldier make, when all you assert supposedly comes from Creo's lips, not your own?"

"You are wiser than you look." Veranna winked. She gathered her long skirts in one hand. "Which way?"

I bit my tongue. "Very well." I would offer no advocacy for this irritating herald of Creo's will. If she faced a contest with the gate-keepers or anyone else, her defense was her own. "Mind that you stay beside me. It would be a shame if you ended up circling the area for days."

Majestrin gave me a wry look before he took to the air once again.

I led the prophetess no more than a quarter mile in the deepening dusk of the forest before the *clomp* of hoof beats reached my ears. From the cover of the undergrowth trotted a pair of sentries, two towering centaurs.

I nodded in greeting. "Hardril, Gaelmoth! Well met, soldiers."

"Captain Ecleriast." Hardril's glance swept me from head to toe. "Our hopes for you to return unscathed seem perhaps in vain?"

"And you come in unfamiliar company." Gaelmoth's grip tightened on the haft of his glaive. "Certainly without those who departed Delsinon beside you."

My gaze dropped to the leaf litter under my feet. "The tale is... long in the telling." I suppressed a groan of welling pain as the centaur's observation stirred the coals of my grief. I squared my shoulders and lifted my chin. "But it shall have to wait for less urgent times. I press for immediate audience with the king."

"I am Veranna, prophetess of Creo," the half-elf said.

I turned a scowl to her interruption of the discourse between the centaurs and me.

Gaelmoth's eyebrow shot up. He muttered something to his partner, in the throaty language of the centaurs. I had always meant to learn their tongue, but never found sufficient time to commit to its study. The two of them exchanged nods, the spark of some realization lighting their eyes.

"Very good," he said, turning back to me. "We shall convey you both through the gates."

Doubly now did I lament the language barrier. What knowledge passed between the guards that gained this outsider such immediate trust?

I shot an accusatory glance at the centaurs. "That is all that you require? A simple giving of a name? Since when are we so casual about the control of our borders?"

"Creo paves the way through even the most crooked of places," Veranna replied.

The throne room of King Saransaeloth glowed with the warm light of braziers. The young king himself sat upon his crystal throne, the flickering firelight playing continually upon its facets in a many-hued dance of hypnotic beauty. He rose as we stepped inside the long hall; Lerendir, his chancellor of war, fell into step beside me as we made our way down the aisle. He passed a glance over my battered armor, a flicker of displeasure darkening his expression.

Let him scowl. Let them all see how hard won this chalice has been.

We progressed past the row of white-barked apple trees that ran down the aisle's center. The scent of the gold apples ripening on the branches filled the air with a heady perfume. The tinkling of Veranna's tiny bells drifted through the chamber, whispering in contrast to the clack of my sabatons as they rang on the marble floor. As we drew near the king of the Delsin, I clasped my fist over my heart and bowed deeply.

"I see you found him," Saransaeloth said.

I furrowed my brow. Did I mishear his greeting?

"Indeed, Your Majesty," Veranna replied. "His quest did not founder in the wilderness."

"Our thanks, Prophetess," Lerendir said.

I folded my arms. "Creo's will?" I snapped. "More like an assignment from my superiors. Charlatan."

Veranna's face blanched. She took a moment to compose herself before saying, "Cannot the will of Creo intertwine with the design of mortals? Indeed, is there anything his creation devises that exists outside of his wisdom?"

I shook my head, stuffing down the string of unwholesome exclamations that threatened to brim over. I reached into my pack and drew out the black Chalice of Gherag-tal. I blew out a breath. "The unwelcome surprise of the journey, Your Majesty. Be advised, I have been warned of some sort of curse perhaps clinging to this thing."

Lerendir took the chalice from me, holding it gingerly between as few fingers as possible. He wrinkled his nose. "Curses, indeed."

He handed the artifact to a steward, who wrapped it in dark cloth.

Lerendir returned his attention to me. "Very good, Captain. You have performed well. Now we can get to the meat of what lies ahead for you."

"Another assignment?" I straightened. The weariness in my muscles would be better driven off by purpose than repose.

"Of sorts." King Saransaeloth rose and took a few steps in front of his throne, his hands clasped behind his back. "As our enemies grow in strength, so must we, if we are to hold them at bay. Veranna has brought it to our attention that Creo wishes to raise up a company of Windriders, under your command, as one facet of this bolstered might."

Young Windrider. Finally, some context.

"So you see," the prophetess said, "I could not let the dragon-kin slaughter you in the mountains. The loss of the chalice would have been tragic, but far less so than the loss of your life, Captain Vinyanel Ecleriast."

Conflict tugged at my spirit. The value of the prophetess's compliment, here in the presence of my liege, was not lost on me, but her probing glance, her ability to know what answers I needed before I had even thought of a question, both nagged me and exposed me. Her apparent misrepresentation of her duties to the king also whispered at the back of my reservations. What did I know about her, really, other than her assertions about herself? And yet, she had gained the confidence of my king and chief commander. It made no sense.

"Creo wills that I should, from the back of a dragon, be an emissary of his justice?"

"And his mercy. It is not for us to choose aspects of such a calling, young Windrider."

I turned to the king and his Chancellor, my gut in sudden turmoil and my cheek hot with flush. "I am...humbled," I said with an effort, "but I shall see this done." *Where to begin?* No amount of compartmentalization training could have kept my trepidation from registering on my face.

"You are strong enough in arms for this duty, Captain," the chancellor said.

"But far too green in spirit," the king added.

The king spoke truth, though I dared not admit it aloud. That did not prevent the lash of its utterance.

I cleared my throat and rocked on my heels. "I attained skill in the ways of the sword at the hands of a mentor. So shall it be with matters of the spirit. I will go to the temple of Creo and—"

The chancellor trod upon my thought. "That will not be necessary. A suitable mentor has already been chosen for you."

I began a mental inventory of the military chaplains, sorting their strengths and wondering which of these elves' experience would most easily adapt to the concerns of a wholly new division, one of such potential magnificence—

"You will begin your study of Creo's will and word under Veranna's tutelage."

Lerendir's words ran me through like a blade. Speechless, I stared at each person in the room in turn until at last, my astonished gaze fell upon the half-elf. Riding upon a dragon instead of a horse? This, I certainly appreciated. Taking on the weighty mantle of my own command of a battalion? Even that, I began to envision. Spending countless hours as a subservient learner to this grating, frail, confusing maiden of dubious parentage?

It appeared the first lesson Creo wished to teach me was humility.

3

BROKEN

MORNING. It always came so early.

I slid several feet down the bench upon which I sat to avoid the beam of brazen sunlight that lanced through the upper windows of the dining hall. I had ample space to choose my seat, since nary an elf sat within three tables of me. And empty the seats around me would remain, since the few elves that would have risked my demeanor at this hour would never again share a breakfast table with me. Our pitched battle with the dragon-kin the day before had ensured that. I sipped my porridge without tasting it, submerged in my bleak sense of loss. *Yesterday I was numb. Today, I am raw.*

Not only did I lack a sense of taste that morning, but my ability to comprehend the spidery script on the parchment that lay beside my bowl also suffered. I had little hope of reading such scrawl through eyes that opened to little better than slits. Grogginess waged a battle upon my intentions, a battle in which I lost ground with each passing moment.

I started at the leathery *thwack* of a book on the table beside me.

"Good morning, Captain."

I gritted my teeth until I could feel the bands of muscle on the sides of my jaw bulging. *Not her. Not now.*

Though I stretched my heavy eyes wider, my clearing vision revealed no improvement in my circumstances. The prophetess Veranna stood beside me, sporting a grin that glared like the winter sun on the surface of snow.

"Morning." I lifted my bowl again and took a long sip.

"I trust your repose was placid and restorative?" she said.

Small talk. Wonderful. "Do I look like it was?"

The prophetess shifted her weight and brushed a wayward tendril of raven hair from her cheek. "Well. Are you ready to learn that which Creo has ordained?" Veranna's singsong tone might just as well have been a mosquito whining beside my ear. Was it not bad enough that the half-elf's irritating mannerisms had plagued my dreams, that now I should have to confront them in waking life?

"Do I have a choice?"

Veranna laughed, the sound of it not unlike the tiny bells that jingled on her riotous attire. "We all have choices before us at every moment, young Windrider." She stepped over the bench beside me and sat. Her straight posture rivaled that of many of the seasoned footmen who dined in the hall around us.

She patted the leather tome she had dropped on the table. "Do you know *The Tree*, Captain?"

"I am familiar with its teachings, yes." I cast my glance to the cracked binding of her copy of the sacred writings of Creo.

Veranna frowned. "Well, if you are to fulfill your calling, you must be not just familiar, but intimate with every word within these pages."

"I shall be certain to peruse a copy at my earliest convenience." My gaze returned to the parchment beside my breakfast bowl. A long pause stretched between us. Without looking up I said, "Are you waiting upon my dismissal?"

The prophetess's already straight spine went rigid. "Are you at all serious about undertaking this training, Vinyanel Ecleriast?"

"I prefer you call me 'Captain,'" I replied. "And yes, I certainly would never pass over the chance to become a commander among my people."

Veranna folded her arms. "Then perhaps you might address the process with a modicum of interest."

"Did not anyone warn you that engaging me over breakfast would prove fruitless? Especially on a morning after I have returned from such grueling toil and loss?"

"They did," Veranna said. "And I chose to ignore such counsel. The will of the Creator waits upon no man, elf, or beast's whim."

I failed to suppress a moan. Again, this emissary of the Creator hamstrung any argument I might make by claiming no ownership of even the words that passed her lips.

"I will not be taught in this moment or in this manner, Prophetess." I stood. "If you wish to pursue this charge Creo has laid upon you, seek me later. Draw upon your own wisdom as to when an elf may have had sufficient time to mourn his fallen comrades."

The lily-white edges of Veranna's pristine nails vanished as she curled her hands into fists. Her face remained dispassionate, but her tight knuckles told the full tale. I had not ascended to my rank of captain of the High Elven Cavalry by stroking those around me with velveted words. I would not practice such delicacy now.

"Captain, Creo will see you to your appointed destiny, whether you follow his lead or stubbornly insist he push you from behind." Veranna gestured to my seat. "Please sit, and I shall offer you guidance on how to glean all you might from *The Tree's* matchless counsel."

I snatched my parchment from the table and shimmied it into a tight roll. "I know how to read, Prophetess. Surely you have not come all this way to teach me something so mundane as that. So take some time—a *lot* of time—to decide upon a lesson more worthy of my attention." I stalked from the dining hall, leaving the half-elven maiden seated beside my unfinished breakfast.

T he sweet scents of grain and timothy hay greeted me as I strode into the stables. Always, that scent brought me a sense of peace, for on those draughts of thick air I smelled dutiful provision being offered the noble animals of my trade. That day, however, the aroma brought with it a biting note. I hesitated before a stall, its door ajar, its clay floor bare of bedding. Absently, my finger traced the carved nameplate that read *Solaris*.

"Captain Ecleriast."

I jumped, quick to swipe away the tears that threatened to brim over and spill down my cheeks.

"At ease, Private," I said, releasing the stable hand from his bow of protocol.

"We did not anticipate your presence today," the young soldier said.

"That is good." A ghost of a smile tugged at my features. "I am glad to see the stables in much the same condition as the days you do expect me."

The soldier relaxed.

"I came to assess the progress with the new colts. Do you have any of them trained yet?" I asked.

"All but one, sir. The sorrel warmblood has molten iron in his veins. We have been able to little more than saddle him."

"Is that so?" I cast a withering glance at the soldier, who shrank beneath it in a satisfying way. "Take me to this thick-headed creature, and we shall see his mettle."

I found the beast in the third wing of the stables, spinning and straining against the cross ties as two grooms fought to saddle him. The commotion of their alarmed cries and the clatter of the colt's hooves raised a din in the aisle that only compounded the headache I had tried to ignore all morning. As the grooms and the horse skittered about in a dance of defiance, the elves waving a bridle at the animal's raised head, I blew a whistle through my teeth that brought all to a standstill.

"Bring me the full bridle," I said. "Once you have, you three are dismissed to whatever remains of your tasks today."

"The full, sir?" one of the grooms asked. My glare sent him bounding for the tack room.

B y midmorning, both the horse and I wore a thick layer of sweat as we stood still in the center of the fortress arena. My stiff fingers protested my grip on the reins. My muscles throbbed from not only the continual exertion of my will against that of the thousand-pound animal, but the many falls I had taken in proving to this creature he had a job to do as a resident of the stables of the Delsin army. Trickling sweat cut pale tracks through the dust and grime on my arms. The horse's flanks heaved behind my calves as he blew through flared nostrils. But when I nudged him with my heels, he stepped forward. Obedient. Collected. A useful, though green, member of my cavalry. Yes, he still needed work, but the horse now knew his place. I gave him a firm pat on the neck.

I reached the edge of the arena. After performing a weary dismount, I handed the reins to the groom who stood nervously behind the fence. "Cool him," I said. "He has worked hard today."

As the horse disappeared to the opposite side of the barn, a chill overran my flesh as a shadow enveloped me. I turned to find Majestrin's gleaming form perched upon the roof of the grandstands, eclipsing the morning sun. Shielding my eyes with one hand, I raised the other in salute to the silver dragon.

He spread his marvelous wings and drifted serenely to the arena floor. The wind that gusted from his landing sent more dirt to cling to my sweaty face.

"You have decided passing Delsinon's walls was worth the risk of arguments or terror?" I said.

"The negotiations were shorter than I expected," Majestrin said. "How did you pass your morning?"

"Breaking a horse." I leaned against his flank, allowing my tired legs a respite.

"Breaking? A curious practice. Why would you want a mount 'broken?'"

I smiled, wiping the grime from my eyes.

Something about Majestrin's presence drove away all but wonder. This was the first moment that day I had fully been able to push aside my grief and anger. "Perhaps you misunderstand the terminology. 'Breaking' simply means to take a wild, unruly animal and teach him how to be useful. How to begin to hear the commands of his master and execute them."

Majestrin cocked his head at me. "So, you mean to say 'training.'"

"Well, no. Not entirely." I sought my mind for the precise words. "The horse I broke this morning surely needs further training, but will likely make a valuable comrade to the rider who takes him into battle someday."

"Valuable? How do you know?"

"His headstrong nature comes only from his intelligence. The smarter the beast, the harder he is to break of his unlearned ways. Yet the greater the reward in the end for both horse and rider."

I had not known Majestrin long, but I began to recognize the expression that overtook his scaly maw as a smile. "And so, even a lesser creature, like a horse, can learn to submit to the wisdom of his betters."

"In the right hands." I hesitated, casting a suspicious glance at the dragon. "How have *you* passed this morning, my reptilian friend?"

"As I said, negotiating." Majestrin lifted the scales on his withers, a sort of draconic shrug.

"You have held council with that insufferable half-elf."

"Only because she sought me. But I had no answers for her frustrations, Captain. It seems Creo arranged his own object lesson between you and this stubborn equine you met with in a contest of wills today."

One quick heave brought me upright from my lean. "Whose ally are you, anyway?"

"Creo's, first and foremost," Majestrin replied. "And most undoubtedly yours. Whatever ways I can help my two friends to work in concert, I shall explore. Even if it means serving as a buffer between a hard-headed soldier and an aggravated prophetess."

I dropped my head back in a skyward glance. With a sigh, I took a few steps from the dragon's side. "This is surreal. I shall look for you another time, then."

"You have a pressing engagement?"

With a rub of my neck, I replied, "I believe I have a protracted appointment with an old book of mine."

After stopping at my quarters to pick up my copy of *The Tree*, I crossed the barracks toward the fortress library. As I passed the gatehouse, the chatter of an assembly caught my notice. Several dozen of the fortress's personnel stood in the bailey between the gatehouse and the open outer gate, and beyond the gate, a stream of elves bearing varied livery paraded by.

Ah, so the competitors for this year's tournament had begun to arrive.

I tucked my book under my arm and strolled toward the crowd.

Those fortress servants who were technically on duty lined the gatehouse and spilled into the middle bailey, some straining on tiptoe to catch sight of the mounted knights riding by. Two Black-watch officers flanked the outer gate, however, as much a reminder for those without as those within where each group belonged.

I restrained a flinch when the major on the left side of the gate made eye contact with me. Curunith's direct superior. I wracked my mind for his name but came up empty. He exchanged a word with his companion and cut a path through the crowd to me.

I clasped my fist over my heart and made a half bow of salute as the major approached.

"Captain Ecleriast?" the major said.

"At your service, sir," I replied.

"Well met. I am Galdurith Emynon of the Blackwatch."

The impending conversation loomed, destined to be awkward. "I believe I know why you have approached me, sir. The details of Curunith's MIA status?"

Galdurith blinked. "If you are at liberty to share them. Though I might also ask *why* he is missing, since you managed to escape to deliver details."

My face tightened. The major blamed me for the loss of one of his decorated personnel? A war between indignance and nausea roiled in my gut.

"My apologies for disappointing you with my survival. I have been back myself little better than a day," I said. "The route Curunith took to provide a diversion would doubtless take far longer, he being on horseback."

Cheers erupted from the crowd around us, as well as a larger, civilian throng beyond the gates. My glance flicked to the bustle, only to catch scarce sight of a silver-armored knight with blue livery passing by on an impressive black charger.

"I could have ascertained that much from the report. So, you agreed to part company?" Galdurith's expression was flinty.

"Traditional tactics had failed to that point," I replied.

A touch on my shoulder—I spun toward it, my heart suddenly pounding.

Veranna took one step back, her hands raised. "Oh dear. I didn't mean to scare you."

I rolled my shoulder and took a breath. Now I truly stood between the hammer and the anvil. "Not at all, Prophetess."

Galdurith raised his eyebrows. Conversation hung like a condemned man awaiting the jolt of the noose.

"Forgive the captain's manners." Veranna stretched a hand toward Galdurith. "I'm Veranna."

Galdurith took her slender fingers in his own black-gloved hand. He smoothed blonde hair back from his forehead with the other. "A pleasure. Major Galdurith Emynon, Blackwatch. And you know each other...how?"

Before I interjected, Veranna replied, "I'm his mentor."

Galdurith failed to suppress a laugh behind closed lips.

Veranna propped a hand on her hip, though her expression remained pleasantly bemused. "You find that funny...Galdurith, was it?"

"Unorthodox, to say the least."

"Well, as I understand it, some soldiers require more unorthodox—"

Veranna clipped her own words with a gasp and a shudder. She drew away from Galdurith's grasp and scuttled toward the outer gate.

We two elves followed.

The prophetess's narrowed glance roved the stream of knights and their entourages progressing up the road.

"What is it?" I asked her.

She continued her search, her nose wrinkled as though a stench filled the air. "Something unseemly. But I've lost it. There's too much other energy clouding my senses." Her glance roved me from head to foot, and she sighed.

I opened my palms to her. "What?"

Galdurith placed a hand on her shoulder. "Not to worry, Prophetess. My soldiers have a long history of ensuring the Week of Tourney remains safe. If anything is amiss, we'll find it."

"Search well, Major," Veranna said. "My hope is that your watchful eye discovers nothing more interesting than my being mistaken."

4

ELIMINATING THE COMPETITION

A MULTICOLORED PALETTE of banners caught high in the after-noon breeze snapped and crackled like the flames of a bonfire. At the south end of the wide arena, practicing trumpeters called to one another through their silver horns, their clarion bell tones raising goose bumps on my skin. Little else brought me the thrill of a tournament. My excitement mounted with every step as I marked off the strides my steed would take as we conquered the field. Once a year, the Week of Tourney dominated the doings of Delsinon. And this year's battle belonged to me.

The stables just outside the contest ring bustled as grooms, stable boys, and warriors prepared their mounts, their partners in competition. A tight cluster of well-dressed elders and officers gesticulated over parchments as they kept a sharp eye to both those who worked the stables and those who, like me, previewed the course for tomorrow morning's first event.

I stood below the rack of rings that awaited my spearing lance. Beside me, a much younger elf, a warrior scarcely beyond boyhood, stared up at the rack.

"They look closer once you are mounted," I said with a smirk.

The youth nearly leapt out of his chain armor. "Yes, sir. I am certain they do, sir. You would know. Sir."

"First tournament?"

The elf swallowed hard. "Is it so obvious?"

"I fear it is." I clapped him on the shoulder. "But take heart. The brave often find favor in this place."

"I hope so. I would not want to embarrass my unit with an unseemly showing—not with..."

The boy's nervous prattle receded into the background of my mind as the prophetess Veranna sashayed up to the cluster of officers outside the ring. What could *she* possibly want? Must she insist upon casting a dark cloud over my one admitted joy?

As she spoke, the entire group turned their gazes to me. Though I did not hear what they said, their conversation certainly *looked* interesting, for vigorous pointing and head shaking punctuated it.

"Sir?"

The voice of the young competitor beside me snapped me away from my ruminations.

"What?"

"I asked if you would compete on the morrow, sir."

I nodded. "Of course. But you will excuse me..." Sparing no glance to the novice, I marched for the railing of the arena.

As the officers saw me coming, three of them scattered to some pressing business. Chancellor Lerendir and the Blackwatch major, Galdurith, remained. And, of course, Veranna.

"Do you find the course well set, Captain?" Chancellor Lerendir asked.

"Verily," I replied. "How go the other preparations? I am anxious for a prompt start at daybreak."

Galdurith cast a raised eyebrow to the chancellor, which he then volleyed to Veranna. A long, agitating silence hung over the group.

"Will you say nothing?" Veranna turned to the others, askance.

The chancellor shook his head. "I know when I cast fuel into a fire, my lady, and I'll not do so here. This decree belongs to you."

Veranna climbed onto the white arena fence and perched on the top rail, a dainty cat poised to preen. "Very well. Captain Ecleriast, you shall not compete in the ensuing festivities."

I guffawed. "No? Just why is that? Shall I spend the week in the library? I have already finished reading *The Tree* from beginning to end."

My words hit Veranna and stuck. I smiled.

She blinked a few times, then cleared her throat. "Excellent, Captain. You are dedicated in your study."

"So, with that settled," I began, clapping the dirt from my hands as I turned toward the gate, "I have some practice ahead of me this evening."

The Prophetess leveled her gaze at me. "No, Captain. You do not. You will not compete this year. By the king's order."

"What?" No mirth laced my words this time. "Is not this tournament to determine his champion? Had battle not called me from the event last year, I would have secured the title then! Surely he does not intend to slight me by denying me my rightful chance—"

"While I'm sure he intends no slight, his order stands, Captain," the chancellor interjected, holding forth a parchment. At the bottom of the flowing script, I saw the undeniable gold seal, the mark of my liege.

I stabbed my burning glance at each of the elves before me, none of whom so much as flinched. "I shall address King Saransaeloth myself over it."

Veranna hopped down from the fence and into my path. She took hold of both my wrists, her touch like the alighting of butterflies. "Vinyanel," she said with a supple softness. "Try to understand. Yes, even without your trusted Solaris, you are the warrior who would win this contest. None deny it. But you cannot be everything at once."

Her delicacy caught me off-guard. In her face, for the first time since I had met her, I saw tender sympathy, and it seared me like a brand. I cursed the lump that rose in my throat as she intoned the name of my lost mount. Setting my jaw, I rolled my eyes skyward. *Welling tears?* I forbade them.

In a whisper no louder than the evening breeze, Veranna said, "Do not cling to what is good and leave yourself no empty hand to accept that which is best, young Windrider."

I wrenched my hands away from the prophetess with greater force than necessary. "Just because I have a duty to pursue this command—a process which I assume will take months—does that mean I should sit, untested, in the meantime?"

A desperate look swept over Veranna's face. "Now, we did not say—"

"I heard enough of what you *did* say, Veranna! Good day." I spun on my heel and stomped off. Major Galdurith glared at me as I passed.

Before I had gone a handful of paces, the chancellor called, "Captain, halt. That is an order."

I brought my feet together, but did not turn.

"Just because you shall not compete, that does not mean you are unneeded," Chancellor Lerendir continued. "This year, you shall officiate."

Officiate? The absurdity grew with every word the elder spoke. Officiating fell to old gray-pates like him. Elves whose sword arm lifted little more than a goblet with any regularity. A litany of infuriated outbursts paraded through my mind, but instead of unleashing one, I sucked my teeth.

I performed the crispest about-face of my lifetime to stare down Veranna and the chancellor from beneath lowered brows. "Yes, sir. Is there anything else?"

"No, Captain. You are dismissed."

After pounding my fists into more than one beam that supported the grandstands, I worked my way around the arena, my mere countenance clearing the path of other elves.

———

T he sharp crack of lance against shield echoed through the arena, compelling the multitudes that packed the grandstands to gasp as one. I dodged the splinters of the riven weapon that flew past my head. One of the two combatants before me tumbled from the back of his horse and landed with a rattling thud on the dirt floor of the arena, kicking up a cloud of caramel-colored dust. I winced for him before I dashed closer to the downed warrior. I had been in his position and did not envy him.

The contestant scrambled to his feet, tossing his lance aside and groping for his sword. The lack of surety with which his hand found his hilt told me who would prevail in this round. He spread his feet shoulder-wide and braced himself to meet the charge of the horseman who came about at the other end of the arena.

The ground trembled under the thundering footfalls of the black courser in blue and silver barding as he charged toward the center of the field of contest. The elf on its back drew a heavy flail, the links of its chain rattling like impish laughter. The mounted warrior brought his weapon around as he bore down upon the footman, and again the clamor of weapon-meets-shield rent the air. This time, pieces of the shield flew all directions, and the footman crumpled to the ground.

The courser careened past me, a little too close for my taste, so I shot a glare at its rider before I raised my hand high. The herald trumpeters blew the Cease of Battle call.

"No, I—I can go on," the footman rasped as he struggled to one knee.

With the gruesome angle at which his forearm hung, I knew his words to be no more than bravado. The healers and I converged upon the downed contestant. His condition looked no better up close than it had from a distance.

"This round is over for you," I said. "Go get that arm straightened out."

As the wounded footman turned for the arena's edge, polite acknowledgment of his efforts rippled through the stands. Unhurried, I headed for the center of the arena. When I turned to face the crowd, I raised my chin to gaze past the multitudes and addressed King Saransaeloth in the royal spectators' box.

"The round goes to Sir Direllian Mithveranon!" I proclaimed for the third time that day.

Thunderous applause erupted from the crowd as Mithveranon made a final circuit of the arena to pass through the gate. Over the past three days this warrior, whose name no one had heard before he first took the field, had proven unbeatable. He showed no lack of prowess. Decorum, perhaps. I did not doubt Mithveranon would stand among the finalists, a contender for the title of king's champion.

The trumpeters burst into a complicated rill, calling the spectators to tea. I smirked at the idea. Having stood amidst every event today, my body bore a thick layer of dirt, the wages of my forced role in this year's tournament. No matter. Those who put me in this position left it quite clear I was to be in attendance. My strides reluctant, I crossed the arena toward the opulent set of tents where overdressed dignitaries and their hangers-on assembled. Puffery and politics. I rolled my eyes. If nothing else, at least there would be shade.

I stepped inside the tent where the officers of Delsinon's fortress took their repose. Before I had even cleared the entry,

Prophetess Veranna swished up to me and handed me a dainty saucer and cup.

"The tea is quite good," she said. "No doubt you are parched."

I repressed a snort at her doting. It would take more than imported tea for her to make amends for what she had done.

Several sergeants crowded me as I took my first sip, wetting a throat dryer than the sands of North Deklia. Their polished insignia proclaimed their divisions: Blackwatch, Wardancers, Cavalry. The officers jockeyed for position, talking over one another as they attempted to lay compliments at my feet.

"His Majesty shall certainly acquire a fine champion this year, with the tournament in your capable hands, Captain Ecleriast."

"A smoothly run operation, Captain. A true pleasure."

"Never has the tournament had such an air of authority—all owing to your leadership."

I nodded in response between sips of tea or mouthfuls of dainties, quietly accepting the accolades—the small spoils of my position.

"So, is officiating such a terrible arrangement?" The corner of Veranna's lip took a crooked upturn. She extended a marble plate of assorted foods to me, all composed as much for color and composition as taste.

I crunched on a point of toast topped with a fried quail's egg. "So far it has been...bearable," I replied. To Veranna's good fortune, my temper over the whole matter had cooled over the past few days.

As teatime wore on, I eventually worked my way to a corner of the pavilion, where a minimal amount of idle gossip from officers' wives reached my ears. One maiden, clad in flowing black, caught my attention as she lingered on the outskirts of the conversation. The dark garb and the haunted look in her eye reminded me why she looked familiar. My last assignment had made her a widow. This I knew. Yet somehow, I could not call to mind the moment that sent her soldier husband to Creo's halls.

Clammy sweat dewed my palms. The more I sought the events of the chalice campaign, the murkier they became. Only flashes of heat, of stone, and the glint of steel came to mind. The sharp tear of claws across my flesh remained all too clear in my muscle memory. But the loss of my squadron? That memory vanished behind a curtain of black. I deposited the remainder of the confection in my hand on a tray.

Just as I began to debate whether I should find a discreet place, should my stomach follow through on its threats to vomit, the trumpets in the arena sounded again. I straightened my tabard, wiped the sweat from my upper lip, and marched through the crowd, destined for the day's final round of jousting. Despite the tinkling that fluttered up behind me, I did not slacken my pace. I neared the grandstands, and Veranna jogged to my side.

"You really are doing an excellent job, Captain," she said. "You let the compliments roll off like rain upon oilskin, but I hope you can glean some sense of satisfaction from your contributions."

I halted as a runner pushing a cart of rubbish cut across our path.

Veranna tilted her head. "Are you all right? You look pale."

"Fine. I am fine." I shook my head. "I find no joy in administration. But I must serve my king, and this role is where he has placed me."

Veranna clapped her hands together. "Exactly! Within that thought lies the very core truth that will draw elves to follow you, no matter what you command. You have proven your supremacy in arms. Perhaps the time has come for you to use your gifts for someone else's benefit and glory."

An air of earnestness and urgency swelled Veranna's words, and something in her imploring tone strummed a chord deep within me.

"The servant shall lead them," I said to the air. *"His greatness shall lie in his abasement. The multitudes shall flock to his humble meekness."*

"There is hope for you yet, Captain." Veranna smiled, and a ray of inner light lanced across her burdened countenance. She opened her mouth to speak again, but a strangled yelp from behind a nearby tent swept her words away. With a furrowed brow, I turned from my path and rounded the tent.

Behind it, a growing pile of refuse loomed. Clearly, the runners deposited all the leavings of revelry here, and the fly-ridden heap had grown quite large in just a few days' time. The runner who had passed us earlier stood in front of the pile, hand clapped over his mouth and eyes squeezed shut. His knuckles whitened around the rake he held in his other hand.

"You all right?" I asked. The rubbish did not smell that bad. Yet.

The runner pointed a shaky finger behind him.

I peered around the young elf. I saw nothing at first besides rinds of melons, crusts of bread, cast-off garnishes, and the bones of standing rib roasts. Then my eyes widened.

Out of the refuse dangled an arm, ash-gray and limp.

Veranna stepped up beside me. "What is it, Cap—" Her jaw fell open, incapable of forming any further words.

I snatched the rake from the runner. With several swipes of the tool, I exposed the shoulder, chest, then face of the unfortunate elf beneath the refuse. The obvious ravages of warm weather on a corpse dead several days distorted the features I saw, but even so, the likeness was unmistakable.

This very deceased elf was a rotting clone of Mithveranon.

5

MITHVERANON'S COLORS

"SIR DIRELLIAN MITHVERANON, please present your writ of acceptance into this year's tournament," I said. The sound of my voice fell dead in the tapestries that lined the walls of the chamber.

The knight, clad in a blue velvet waistcoat embroidered with a wolf's head, swallowed hard. He produced a folded parchment from the pouch on his belt and stepped forward.

I reached across the walnut desk before me and took the document. He smiled as I unfolded it, an uneasy half grin.

After I opened the parchment, I scanned the document in silence. Mithveranon pursed his lips. Dropped his gaze to the floor. Rocked back on his heels. To his credit, he did not speak.

I passed the parchment to a runner behind me. "Convey this to the Blackwatch headquarters."

The page nodded. "Indeed, sir." He slipped from the room on quick strides.

"By all appearances, you seem ill at ease," I said to Mithveranon.

He cleared his throat. "My apologies, sir, but considering how I've trained for this tournament—the years I've put in...have I somehow misstepped and jeopardized that?"

"Tell me where you come from." I sat in the chair on my side of the desk and picked up a quill.

"My family hails from the elven quarter in the port city of Myslapten, our estates being on Dirthannan, held there for six generations." His voice quavered, but only slightly. "My father is a member of the elite guard there, and my mother, sadly, passed just twelve years ago."

"My sympathies," I said. "Of what?"

Mithveranon blinked. "Come again?"

"Your mother. Her cause of death?"

"Oh." Mithveranon swiped a handkerchief across his alabaster brow. "She was slain by zealots who condemned her Thaumaturgy as witchcraft."

I dipped the quill and made a quick note of his answer. "Have you petitioned to compete in the tournament in past years?"

"Only once, sir, but my petition was rejected because the courier service I hired failed to deliver it in time. I hand-carried my documents this year, as far as Earannon, to ensure no such mistake happened again."

I continued to serve up questions about Mithveranon's background, about his doings since he arrived in Delsinon, and his plans for his return home, which he answered with nervous speed, his fists clenching and unclenching all the while. We surveyed his extended family, yet I found no individual within it of similar age to him or matching gender.

The door to the chamber opened. Mithveranon turned, and I rose. Upon seeing Veranna standing in the doorway, I plunked into my seat again.

"Not now, Veranna. I'm not finished here."

She breezed into the room. "This must be Direllian."

Mithveranon's gaze crawled over the prophetess at a slow, oozy pace. "Veranna, is it?" He extended a hand.

Veranna placed her fingers in Mithveranon's grasp. She shivered when he pressed them to his lips.

"I mean it," I said. "I am in the middle of questioning. Where should I seek you afterward?"

After wrapping one of her scarves a little tighter around her shoulders, Veranna met Mithveranon's gaze. "How schooled are you in Thaumaturgy, Direllian?"

He smiled. "I've neglected it in favor of swordplay, but I'm sure I could be persuaded to give it better attention, were I placed beneath the right tutor."

Veranna folded her arms. "I see."

I stood. "Have a care, Mithveranon. You stray too close to predatory—"

"Per section fourteen of the Knight's Code, Behavior Unseemly to a Knight, subsection five," Mithveranon said, "A knight will not engage in predatory behavior toward the opposite sex, neither in implication nor actions."

"See that you apply your knowledge," I said.

Mithveranon lifted his palms in surrender. "Oh, I understand. I'd be territorial if I had a rover girlfriend too."

Veranna's jaw fell slack, and her eyes narrowed.

"Her ability to effectively advise me in spiritual matters would suffer greatly if I opted to call on her as well." I quarter-turned to Veranna. "Which I assure you has never been a risk."

Mithveranon chuckled into his fist.

The rap of knuckles on the doorframe commanded my notice. Major Emynon stood in the doorway.

"What in the Maker's Dominion makes you think you can just open an investigation with none of my people involved, Ecleriast?" the major said.

I sighed. "This is tournament business, Major, which falls under the jurisdiction of the head officiate, until I deem otherwise."

"Speaking of which, don't you have a tournament to complete?" The major ground his teeth.

"Indeed," I replied. "So the sooner I can finish here, without interruptions, the sooner I can attend to my assignment there."

Mithveranon's glance bounced around the room. "Have I done something wrong that I'm unaware of? I don't even know what this line of questioning has been about."

"We are not yet at the point where we can be more transparent about the situation that has prompted the questioning, Mithveranon," I said.

"Will it affect my eligibility for the final tomorrow?" A dew of sweat beaded on Mithveranon's brow.

"Any more audacious behavior or inappropriate insinuations, and it just might." I glared at him from beneath lowered brows.

The major set his jaw. "Captain, a word, please?" He jerked his thumb toward the door.

I rose and picked up the notes I had drafted. "Please excuse us for a *brief* moment." After rounding the desk, I hooked Veranna's arm and led her from the room, just behind the major.

He closed the door once we all stood in the hall.

I shoved the notes into the major's chest. "I do not appreciate you barging into my proceedings and casting an air of inauthenticity over what I am trying to accomplish."

His eyes widened. "Inauthenticity? What do you know about questioning a person of interest?"

"Review my notes, Major, and you decide if I failed to gather the pertinent information," I said.

"You can be sure I will," the major said. "But until I have, I order that you suspend this inquiry and stick to swords and lances like you've been asked. This really doesn't concern you."

I lowered my voice to a punctuated whisper. "One of my competitors, the one who looks very likely to win the title of king's champion, appears to be both dead and alive. How does that not concern me?"

Veranna laid a light hand on my shoulder. "Captain. You've

done all you can for now. Let it go—Galdurith's people can expand the investigation from here."

I blew a long breath. Tension crept through my shoulders and neck. "On the condition they keep someone on Mithveranon's tail at all times. I refuse to be the first officiate to crown a fraudulent champion."

6

FIGHT OR FLIGHT

"MY LORD?"

A reptilian figure raised his blood-red eyes from map he contemplated upon the table before him. His scales, the mottled green-gold of tarnished brass, put forth a dull gleam in the torchlight that illuminated his tent, his temporary lair.

"What do you need, Lieutenant?" he answered, his gravelly voice hardly above a whisper. He leaned back in his chair.

"There are new developments in the situation with the Chalice of Gherag-tal, Lord Scitherias," the lieutenant replied, dropping the deep cowl of his cloak behind him. He leaned upon the table, his palms spread on the smooth coolness of the wood.

Lord Scitherias lowered an icy glare at the lieutenant. "Don't scratch my furniture with those ragged brambles you call claws."

The scales on the back of the lieutenant's neck rose like hackles, but he shifted his weight away from the table to clasp his hands behind his back. Why his lordship insisted upon outfitting his quarters with furniture of man-make, the lieutenant never fathomed.

"Now, what of these...developments, you say?"

"It seems the infidels have discovered the body, my lord."

If his lordship was surprised, it certainly didn't show. He tilted his head. "Already, Lieutenant? To whose slipshod craft do we owe this untimely...inconvenience?" His words slipped through the long file of pointed teeth that lined his narrow maw like a serpent slips through grass.

"We assigned the task to one of the Summoned, my lord. Bloodthirsty he was, but apparently not thorough." The lieutenant lashed his spiked tail.

"Well, what else? What do the softbellies do about it?"

"Other than conceal the death from their own kind, it seems little, your lordship. But we thought it would be best to keep you apprised, in case this oversight alters the plan."

The torchlight guttered as the tent flap opened. Both draconic figures who stood within turned their attention to the newcomer, a tall, broad-winged member of the dragon-kin, who wore a complicated array of armor plates in addition to the natural protection of his own garnet scales.

"Lord Scitherias, a word, if I may?" the warrior began, genuflecting deeply as he spoke.

"Why not, Khagrosh?" His Lordship twirled a casual hand in the air. "It's not as though I have gotten the chance to plot any of our next maneuvers with the continual interruptions in camp this evening."

The lieutenant flicked his tongue out the front of his mouth, tasting the air. The warrior brought with him the salty whiff of uncertainty.

"There has been a sighting of what the scouts guess to be a dragon in flight. Some leagues to the south, but closing," the warrior said.

"Is that so? Interesting timing, to say the least." Lord Scitherias focused his attention on the lieutenant for a long, tense moment.

"This could be purely coincidental," the lieutenant replied. His scales emitted a faint chatter as his muscles coiled. "Warrior Khagrosh's report is incomplete, at best."

Lord Scitherias stalked toward the lieutenant, each slow step falling upon the earthen floor of the shrinking space with ominous intent. "You should know by now that I dismiss any assumption of...coincidence."

The lieutenant, however, would not be cowed so easily. He kept his gaze fixed on Lord Scitherias's slit pupils through every ponderous step. "We don't even know what sort of dragon, with all due respect, your lordship. Who knows how many of the creatures the softbellies harbor in their lands?"

"Well," Lord Scitherias continued, his low tone rumbling toward the lieutenant like distant thunder. "Perhaps you and your squadron ought to go make sure the appearance of this dragon is as unimportant as you hope."

My eyes watered with the continual rush of the night wind in my face, but the matchless view of the distant lands below, as well as the dome of bright stars above, more than compensated me for such a small discomfort. In armor, my visor would serve to shield my eyes. I made a mental note that helmets with visors would be a necessary uniform piece for my future battalion.

After several consecutive nights of practice flights with Majestrin, I had finally developed a secure seat, his banks and turns now nearly second nature. The longer we flew, the more I glimpsed my distorted reflection in each of his convex silver scales, the deeper my realization I could never have earned this privilege of dragon-riding. Creo blessed me richly indeed to bestow upon me such a fierce joy.

"What now, Vinyanel, with the Week of Tourney behind

you?" Majestrin asked, his voice both a sound and a sensation as I gripped his sides with my legs.

"Given the rein to pursue more digging on Mithveranon, I would have done that." I sighed. "As I understand it, the Blackwatch are currently chasing after hypotheses ranging anywhere from adultery cover-ups to dimensional rips that have created duplicate elves."

Majestrin snorted. "I wish them luck with either of those. And you had no sense that the 'live' Mithveranon used any questionable means to beat his opponents?"

"Not in the least," I said. "His technique was clean, and he leveraged only small mistakes by his opponents to his advantage."

"It sounds to me like you have all the time you need at present to work on your leadership skills, then. What's your next step for that?" Majestrin said.

"More study with Veranna, I suppose." It came out more begrudged than I had intended.

"I don't envy you. Has she grown any less shrill?"

"A bit. She hardly shrieks at all when she is on the ground." I shrugged. "Though I should be fair. She has tempered her habit of staring down her nose as a 'holy servant of a high God' of late."

"Why the change?"

"Who can say? While she is more tolerable, she remains enigmatic," I replied. "Perhaps her dead faint over finding the body in the rubbish has humbled her a fraction."

Majestrin's sides pulsed, and the series of squawks that emitted from his mouth struck me as laughter.

"Though I will not deny it was awkward when she awoke. I am...unused to frailty at the sight of death. A soldier's life deals out corpses as frequently as daily rations."

"Perhaps Creo demands a mote of tenderness within that soldier's breast," the dragon said.

I hoped he felt my glare boring into the back of his head.

After a few more wing-beats, Majestrin slammed to a stop. I grappled his neck. A few days earlier, I might have pitched from his back entirely.

"Heaven and earth, Majestrin, what are you—"

"Hush!" the dragon said with a hiss. He sniffed several times while he glided in a circle. With a curve of his neck, he turned his brilliant green eyes to me. "Captain, I believe we may have a problem."

Between the shock of his abrupt stop and the affront of his interruption, my humor had gone sour. "Out with it, then. No conundrums."

"I smell dragon-kin on the wind. Either there are many, or they are close."

"How close could they be? You can smell them from this height?" I blustered.

"Well, Captain, they *can*—"

An impact like a catapult stone barreled into me, knocking me clear of Majestrin's back. The terrifying sense of freefall buffeted the breath from my lungs, preventing the scream that would have come otherwise. If I lived through this, I would order the construction of custom tack and barding for Majestrin. With restraining belts.

The dark carpet of treetops below rushed toward me at an alarming rate. Another impact stole my sense of orientation as my body made, as best I ascertained, a lateral lurch. I struggled against the pressure around my midsection. The vibration of a wordless grunt that enveloped my torso snapped me to my senses: Majestrin had caught me in his maw and clenched me ever-so-gingerly to keep his teeth from piercing my flesh. Of all the days to forego wearing my armor.

We careened toward the forest canopy, but this was no easy descent like I had ridden through in the past. Majestrin spun, dove, and banked. Up, down, forward, and back lost all meaning.

What remained of my dinner threatened to evacuate my stomach.

The dragon wheeled a full one hundred and eighty degrees and lifted me high as he lashed out with one of his foretalons. His fearsome claws connected with a smaller winged figure that spun crazily from the force of the attack. A drawn weapon glinted in the figure's hand. My lingering vertigo prevented me from gathering more than that.

Majestrin craned his neck around and plopped me at his withers once more. "Try to stay seated. The ride's going to be rough."

Going to be? I groped around the dragon's back and neck, at a loss for a significant handhold. I clutched one of his dorsal plates and prayed.

With a mighty thrust of his wings, Majestrin surged forward.

"Are we fleeing?" I yelled over the wind that roared in my ears. "How bad is the situation?"

"I simply hope to buy us some time to think. At least two dragon-kin want our hides."

I glanced around the deep cobalt landscape below and caught sight of our two flying opponents, whose wings flapped crazily as they fought to match our speed. It would take a heroic effort, given that Majestrin outsized them at least five-to-one.

Not far ahead, I also spied the spire of a dead tree, mostly stripped of branches from many years of withstanding the press of the elements.

"Majestrin, would you swoop down and break off a couple of fathoms from that tree trunk?" I asked.

The dragon spared a glance back to me, just long enough to offer a devilish grin. "Hold on tight."

He tucked his wings and plummeted in a steep dive. I hunkered down low, putting as much of my torso against his neck as possible so the sheer force of the wind did not tear me from his back. As the leaves of the trees crackled and whipped at Majestrin's hind legs and tail, then came a lurch and a sharp crack. We shot for the sky again.

"Will this do?" Majestrin called, reaching back to hand me the slender tree trunk he had acquired.

I weighed the length of it against my strength. While a little crooked, the shaft mimicked the length and girth of a lance. "Yes, nicely. Come about, my friend."

As we wheeled in a wide arc, I again uttered a brief prayer to Creo. *Almighty Creator, it is going to take nothing short of a miracle to keep me on Majestrin's back in just a few seconds. I leave that up to you.*

The silver dragon thrust toward the approaching dragon-kin, and I singled out the figure on the left, for lack of any educated reason to choose one over the other. The enemy's eyes rounded, and his wing flaps faltered as we bore down upon him. I lowered my tree-trunk-turned-lance, leveling it at my opponent. His hesitancy turned to panic. Limbs and wings flailing, he fought against his own momentum. He had chosen a change of course too late.

With practiced precision, I leaned in and caught him full in the chest with the lance. The impact reverberated down my arm and deep into my core. I had never hit anything that hard or that fast in my life, and yet, even against the jarring slam I had endured, my legs gripped Majestrin's sides like a blacksmith had forged us into a single entity. The lance snapped as the speared dragon-kin dropped from the sky.

The speed and force of the hit should have thrown me from Majestrin's back. Lesser blows had launched me from the saddle on plenty of occasions, but at least then, I had known how to roll and regain my feet. As the rush from engagement ebbed, an arc of pain radiated from my tailbone.

I glanced behind me. The lance strike had rammed my posterior against one of Majestrin's tall dorsal plates, and I had no doubt I would carry an enviable bruise, at the least. High-cantled saddles. Also an equipment requirement for windriding.

"Where's the other?" I called to Majestrin.

"He dropped into a dive right before you skewered his companion," Majestrin said.

He turned again, and I scanned the sky for our second foe. What remained of my lance might serve as a quarterstaff. Our quick victory over our first opponent emboldened me just enough to give it a try.

"We need the second brute alive, if we can get him," I said to the dragon. "I should like a chance at persuading him to divulge what brought him and his friend so far south. So, if we spot him, do me a favor and do not swallow him in one gulp."

"Perish the thought." Majestrin shuddered beneath me. "I have a personal dictum that I shan't eat anything that talks, evil or not."

I chuckled darkly. "Let us keep that little matter to ourselves, at least for the time being."

I sought our surroundings for the remaining enemy, thankful that the darkness was no obstacle to my sight. A rustle of canopy caught my eye.

"There!" I pointed down to the spot.

Majestrin plummeted toward our quarry, and I grimaced in anticipation of the assault of the tree branches on my flesh. The dragon-kin tore recklessly through the growth, but we still closed upon him in little time.

When his black boots touched the forest floor, the reptilian fiend broke into a run. We charged after him. A maniacal war cry erupted from my mouth as we hunted him; he had no hope of outpacing us.

The creature burst into a clearing and whirled to face us, his crimson-lined cape flaring dramatically around him. Could he truly be so foolhardy? Did he really dare face down not only me, but a mature silver dragon? His last stand would be a short one.

We crashed into the clearing as well, when from the opposite side of the dense tree cover, a score or more dragon-kin stepped from the shadows, weapons drawn. My assurance melted away.

If ever I saw a need for prayers, this was it.

7

ALONE

MAJESTRIN and I silently faced the rank of twenty dragon-kin that stood before us, framing the far side of the clearing. Some carried bare-bladed swords, glistening cold in the moonlight. Others hefted axes; yet others, maces or bolas. I looked down at my clenched fists. What did I wield? A broken stick. At least it was pointy.

A guttural croak boomed from the throat of the reptilian creature in the center of the group. They charged.

Majestrin's ribs expanded beneath my legs in a sudden gulp of air, much deeper than a normal breath. He reared with such suddenness that I flung my arms around his neck to keep my seat. The dragon thrust his head toward the advancing line of enemies, and a devastating cone of white burst forth from his maw. No fewer than a dozen of our foes writhed, engulfed in the deadly cold, their piercing screams cut short by sudden death. The shriveled remnants of their frozen remains toppled onto the ground and crumbled on impact. As Majestrin dropped his foretalons to the ground again, I found our odds of surviving this battle much improved.

My assurance evaporated more quickly than the curling

tendrils of mist rising from our frozen opponents. Out of the gloom surrounding the clearing, another score of enemies emerged.

"Blast!" Majestrin said from between clenched teeth.

"Yes, please do!" I replied.

"I wish I could. But it takes a—"

The onslaught of the dragon-kin reinforcements cut off Majestrin's explanation. They swarmed in with whoops and croaks. Tonight, would I depart this mortal plane, to join my friends who had fallen to the merciless attacks of these villains? Not without a fight.

It had been a long time since I had taken the blow of any weapon without the protection of armor, so when the first set of bolas flew, wrapped around me, and battered my ribs, my eyes flew wide. I grunted involuntarily. Another set, then another found their mark on my head and torso.

Majestrin scuttled to the side, dodging the whistling blades of the sword- and axmen. His tail swept in arcs that scattered our foes. All the while, he gulped in repeated deep breaths. He dared not unfurl the membranous expanse of his wings, his only area of vulnerability, as far as I saw.

I swung the remnants of my makeshift lance, driving off a few of my attackers despite my partial entanglement and the enemies' force of numbers.

A throwing ax hurtled my way, and while I saw it soon enough to duck it, my movement opposed Majestrin's, and I pitched from his back. Would the dragon trample me in his frenzy? Or prone, would I meet my end at the blades of the enemy? Both presented as likely a future.

I hit the undergrowth of the clearing and, to my surprise, no legion of blades dived in to vivisect me. Instead, the black webbing of a net obscured my vision. I flailed in one last desperate hope to avoid capture, but the dragon-kin were too swift. They dragged me clear of Majestrin, and though from the ground I saw little more than a legion of scaled legs, crocodilian tails, and capes, they clearly circled around me, packed tight.

Above the chaos, my dragon mount again reared high, towering thirty feet above the fray. He took one final, deep breath, but when his battle-crazed gaze met mine, ensnared in the midst of the dragon-kin pack, his lungs deflated, and the barest trickle of ice-cold vapor drifted from his maw.

A mocking chuckle rumbled through the pack of brigands around me. Ringing me three soldiers deep, they braced polearms against an assault from any side. Their strategy grew clear to me: they gambled that Majestrin would not breathe his deadly burst of cold on them if the stroke would kill me too. They won that wager.

The dragon eyed the steel thicket of blades that surrounded me.

In the moment of stillness, I bellowed, "Majestrin, get out of here!"

Majestrin stepped back, his eyes bewildered and pained. I did not have time to explain. Another rider, my people could find. Another dragon, willing to bear him? Unlikely.

"Go! NOW!" I roared.

A steely look overtook Majestrin's face as the frontmost of the dragon-kin warriors shook the hafts of their weapons, taunts spilling from their lips. For a moment, I feared he would make a foolish stand. But instead, he lifted his wings, already battered, and launched into the sky. The crowd around me cheered before a sharp blow to the back of my head plunged me into darkness.

Veranna wended her way through the throng of elvenkind that clogged the lawn around Delsinon's fortress; young and old raised their glasses to newly established King's Champion Sir Direllian Mithveranon. Every time a cheer rose up in the warrior's honor, she shuddered. Yes, the Blackwatch, the king's elite intelligence agency, had done a matchless job of keeping quiet the news of the body discovered on the tournament grounds, yet they had unearthed little else in their flurry of investigation. Did anyone else at the night's festivities share her clawing sense of unease at the mystery that remained unsolved? Somehow, every time she looked at the champion's broad grin, she more so beheld the death grimace of the corpse in the rubbish.

She cast her glance to the height of the moon as it made its nightly voyage across the summer sky. Soon enough, Vinyanel should arrive for his next lesson in Creo's statutes. It was as good an excuse as any other to slip away from the crowd in which she stood. While amidst the throng, she felt no part of it. Interesting that Vinyanel should choose to pursue work while the whole of Delsinon reveled. When would he find he could no longer bury his grief in business and bravado?

Veranna pressed through the revelers to make for the fortress itself. She fought to ignore the way the mothers in the crowd steered their children as far from the half-elven prophetess as the space allowed. She turned a stoic cheek to the disdainful sneers that jabbed from the eyes of the venerable elves she passed. She lifted her chin high, making no apology for her parentage. Her years among elves and men had shown her worse rejection than this.

The fortress itself, nearly emptied by the festivities outside, offered some respite. Only her footfalls on the marble floors, the rustle of her skirts and scarves, and the occasional muffled hurrah from outside spoke to her within the walls. Up, up, up the spiral stairs of the north tower carried her, until she reached the door to the battlement. Veranna laid her hand upon the scrolling iron handle, gripping the cool metal for one moment, then another. Only after a deep breath and a smoothing of her hair did she push the portal open.

She stood in the doorway, staring across the moon-bathed walkway. Though the floor was certainly wide, the parapet to her left...why did it have to be so low? One careless lean would pitch even a person of her diminutive stature over the edge. Perhaps the captain had set this battlement as their meeting place out of pure spite. He knew her weakness for heights. With a grit of her teeth, she strode out into the blue light of the moon.

Her gaze did not so much as touch upon the winking lanterns and riotous colors of the festival below. Creo help Vinyanel should he not appear soon.

Veranna hugged her arms around her middle as the evening breeze snaked its way through her clothing, sending a chill up her spine. Odd, on a balmy summer night. The barest whisper of breath turned the prickling chill to a shiver, and Veranna whirled around, her hands thrust out in front of her to ward off whatever danger might approach.

A figure, dressed in black from chin to heel, leaned against the fortress wall she now faced. The tall building cast him in shadow, though Veranna saw him buff his nails against the pile of his waistcoat. Her muscles, tight as a bowstring, relaxed.

"Is that you, Major?" she breathed.

The figure pushed away from the wall and took several soundless strides toward her.

"It is." He reached out toward Veranna.

She slipped her hand into his, the caramel tones of her own fingers shockingly dark against the paleness of his, but she concealed her reaction as he brushed her hand with his lips. Of all the elves she had met in Delsinon, so far only Major Galdurith treated her as a lady of his own kind.

"What brings you up here?" Veranna asked.

"I might have made the same inquiry to you, Prophetess." He released her hand and cast her a small, lopsided smile.

"I await Captain Ecleriast." Veranna searched the sky. "He has studying to do, and he set this as the rendezvous point this evening. What about you?"

"I stand on duty." The major took a few purposeful strides along the parapet. "It has been a dull post. Until now."

Veranna smoothed a tendril of hair over her ear. She cleared her throat. "Any new developments with the research about the surname Mithveranon?"

The major's smile dissolved. "None. It will be some time before we receive any communication from the family that registered a competitor for Tourney. News travels slow from our annexes in the northern ports."

"And they may be reticent to reveal any missing information in their genealogy," Veranna said. "There may be a scandal at stake."

"If a scandal among northern nobles is all that this situation uncovers, I'll call it good fortune," Galdurith said.

"You suspect something else?" Veranna intercepted Galdurith's distant gaze.

"Your assessment that Mithveranon has magical inclinations troubles me," Galdurith said. "It casts quite a fog over the field, so to speak."

"Indeed." Veranna glanced down to the center stage of the festival, where Sir Mithveranon shook countless hands. The four-story drop made her stomach lurch, so she averted her gaze.

"Well," the major continued, "I hope your study time with the captain does not overtax even your measure of patience, Prophetess. You seem set up for quite a trial there, in my mind."

"All pursuits that stand to bear such an immense harvest come with hardship, Major," Veranna replied. "I await the glorious testimony that will surround whatever Creo makes of the unruly Captain Ecleriast. I grow more thankful that the task does not lie in my hands alone."

The major chuckled. "You're no soldier. Please, call me Galdurith."

Veranna's stomach fluttered. "I would never presume—"

"It's not presumption when you've been extended the invitation." He met Veranna's gaze. "And you don't have to recite your script with me, if you don't want. I imagine you have few confidants in this city."

More like none. But I'm used to that. Veranna summoned a smile. "Your offer is a kind one, but..."

Galdurith's focus lingered over her shoulder, and his face tightened.

"What is it?" Veranna turned. Her last stride wobbled as she neared the wall's edge.

"Ah, our time together is cut too short." Galdurith pointed into the night sky. "If I am not mistaken, it appears your wayward student rushes to the schoolhouse now."

Veranna followed the major's outstretched finger with her gaze. A dark shape blotted out a few of the distant stars. For several long moments, she watched the shadow in the distance grow until even she could see the beating wings and lithe body of the dragon, reflecting the moonlight. Majestrin closed on the keep, circling it as he scanned the structure. He whipped his head back and forth, searching.

Veranna stood on tiptoe and waved her hand above her head. Why would the dragon look so unsure of where to land? Vinyanel himself had set the place of meeting. The prophetess stared more intently at Majestrin.

He was alone. No rider.

Majestrin banked sharply to fly straight toward her. With a gusty flap of his wings that sent wavy tresses across Veranna's face, he eased onto the battlement. The perch seemed precariously insufficient for his girth and length. Now that he was close, Veranna heard his breath coming in great gasps, like wind rushing through an enormous bellows.

"Where is Vinyanel?" Veranna said.

"Alas, Prophetess." The dragon continued to gulp great

draughts of air, creating an ebbing and flowing breeze atop the battlements. "He's in a...mess—terrible mess..."

"Oh, is that so?" Galdurith said, betraying no more sense of alarm than might be conveyed by the arch of an eyebrow. "So the talented Captain Ecleriast is fallible, contrary to what I've been told. What's he gotten himself into?"

Majestrin shot a quick, black look at the major, but then turned attention back to the prophetess. "I took him on a little flying lesson. Fully—fully intended to have him back for his appointment. But some leagues to the north...dragon-kin. Ambushed us." Majestrin's sides continued to heave, but slowed as he spoke.

"Ambushed? Where is the captain?" Veranna blurted.

"Dragon-kin? In the elf-lands?" the major said at the same moment.

"It is far by land—just beyond the forking of the Nuruhain and Arin...but I think we can make it back in time." Majestrin glanced to the sky.

Veranna hesitated, unsure of which part of Majestrin's response to address first. *We? In time for what?*

Majestrin lowered his wing to the walkway. Veranna's every horrifying memory of the flight to Delsinon flooded her mind, and the palpable sensation of the color draining from her cheeks sent a chill down her neck.

"Surely, Majestrin, we ought to take some time to strategize." Veranna's tongue clung to the roof of her dry mouth. "We need to send the right elves to handle this situation if we hope to succeed."

"My thoughts exactly." Galdurith briskly piled his words on top of Veranna's. "I will notify my unit, and we can assemble a reconnaissance team—"

"And *march* all the way to Vinyanel's location?" Majestrin shot back with a snap of his jaws. "By the time your team arrives, you'll find naught but Vinyanel's blackened bones!" The dragon leveled his gaze at Veranna. "If you insist on dalliance, I shall return on my own. The dragonsbond compels me. Though I had hoped to have your help."

Galdurith gaped. "You're a dragon. If you know where Vinyanel has been taken, you had no means of recovering him?"

"The dragon-kin, both in the ambush and in their encampment, were uncannily prepared to defend against my abilities," Majestrin said. "My kind is powerful, but not impervious."

Galdurith blustered before forming cohesive words. "Encampment? Something dire is afoot here."

Veranna closed her eyes, raising her face to the heavens and stretching her arms wide. The evening breeze filtered through her clothes and jingled the silver bells that dangled from every hem and corner. Her mood shifted from placid, almost blank, to resolute—though her stomach roiled beneath it all.

"I will go. Creo's Virtusen are our chief hope to succeed in this rescue."

Galdurith pursed his lips. "Virtusen?"

Veranna's slow steps carried her to Majestrin's side, and she clasped her hands as she walked, though it scarcely masked their trembling. "Specific acts of magic performed in accordance with Creo's will." Whether she relished the idea of flight again or not, something deeper than even Majestrin's oath to Vinyanel insisted she help.

The major cracked his knuckles as Veranna took shaky hold of Majestrin's wing. The elf strode to her side. "Do you have a plan? If you would give me just a moment to assign another guardsman to my post, I could help you."

"I will lose no further time, elf of the Blackwatch," Majestrin said. "Follow north if you can, but I expect your business will be more about uncovering the meaning behind these enemies' presence than anything else."

"Veranna, this is madness," Galdurith said.

"I know." She hoisted herself toward Majestrin's back, but

struggled for a foothold before she had climbed halfway. "But oftentimes, it's apparent madness that sets a choice apart from a calling."

Galdurith shook his head, a sympathetic smile on his lips. He clasped Veranna's waist and gave her a gentle boost to her lofty seat upon the dragon.

"Creo speed you on your rescue." His brow furrowed. "I don't like sending you alone."

Veranna smiled despite the roiling flutter in her stomach. "Alone? I never am, Galdurith. I never am."

8

RUDE AWAKENING

MUFFLED SOUNDS DRIFTED TO ME, garbled and nonsensical as if they came through deep water. I could not tell if the noise came from my fitful nightmares or from my surroundings, for reality slipped through my fingers like sand. Time passed unmarked; the sounds grew in clarity, but I simply lay still and listened. My relentless nausea refused me the ability to do otherwise. My head throbbed. What did I hear? Beasts? The guttural croaking that rambled behind me, too organized for mere animals, grasped my memory by the shoulders and shook.

Of course! The snarling language of dragon-kin—I knew that sound. It was no dream.

I dared part my eyelids. Thickened and crusted, they clung to my eyes. The room whirled at first, and I tensed my muscles against the inevitable eruption of my churning gut. But no, the dim space around me slowed to a stop.

I lay on my side, my hands and feet bound, facing the taupe canvas wall of what appeared to be a tent. In the corner, I spied a highly polished silver shield, in whose convex surface I saw the interior of the tent behind me—a stroke of luck in regrettable circumstances. The shield reflected the image of two dragon-kin,

and judging by the sound of their croaks and their wild gesticula-
tions, they debated. I knew a scant few words of their language,
but one word that kept emerging, there was no mistaking.

Queldurik.

The false god of the demon worshipers of the north. The
entity to which live sacrifice by burning was the chief act of
adoration. One of the dragon-kin said the name with insistence,
the other with dismissive disdain.

One of the dragon-kin, a creature with tarnished, brassy
scales, the one who scorned Queldurik's name, broke from the
conversation. His figure stretched and warped in the shield's
reflection as he approached, until the colors of his rich garb filled
its surface. A sharp, armored toe kicked into my back.

"You awake, softbelly?"

I stifled my grunt at the deliberate shot to my vitals and
responded through gritted teeth. "No."

The dragon-kin bent and clutched the front of my tunic with
his claws. He hauled me to a sitting position, an awkward
maneuver that grated my face across the sisal weave of the mat on
the floor. Sitting awoke a sharp reminder of the bruising I had
taken during my earlier in-air tilt. The creature's blue-black
tongue flicked out the front of his snout as he bored into me with
slit pupils.

"Amusing. I recommend you awaken, or I shall leave you to
the zealots who think no further than to see you burn."

I steeled my expression, as war had taught me, for I recognized this villain, even if he failed to recognize me. How could I
forget the wielder of powerful curses that had consumed so many
of my lost squadron? My blurring vision, the green churning that
crept up my throat and under my tongue, my unnerving confusion—all these warred against my front line of stoicism, but I
dared not falter now. Especially since I failed to recall how I had
come to be in Lord Scitherias' clutches.

"Now, we shall converse, and I do hope you choose cooperation. I tire of the girlish shrieks that your kind makes under duress."

I swallowed the bile in my throat. "I have few words to waste on you, Scitherias." I looked up and down the dragon-kin's plush burgundy waistcoat and the supple sable of his breeches, altered to accommodate his three-foot tail. "Playing dress-up like a man, but too repugnant to be counted among their kind. And yet, too feeble to stand among true dragons—"

A sharp crack of Scitherias's knuckles across my face cut my insults short. The metallic taste of blood pooled beside my tongue. I turned back to him with narrowed eyes, though I am sure I swayed with the reeling in my head.

"I shall give you one chance, softbelly." Scitherias leaned in close. The acrid smell that always hung about the dragon-kin filled my nostrils. "Who scouts our position with you?"

"No one."

Scitherias drove the heel of his hand into my nose before I even flinched. Stars burst across my vision and a hot gush ran down my lip. I fought to divorce myself from my circumstances. Chances were, they would only grow worse before the dragon kin tired of beating answers from me.

"As you can imagine, I have much more creative individuals at my disposal to extract this information from you." Scitherias rose and marched to the tent opening. "A shame I can't call it a pleasure seeing you again, Captain Ecleriast."

———

M ajestrin tore through the night sky as Veranna clung to his neck, eyes squeezed shut and too terrified to even scream. The lurching of his body as he thrust his wings against the air threatened to throw her from his back at any moment. She long ago refused to look upon the world that had receded so astonishingly far below.

A gust of high-altitude wind knocked against the dragon, and he banked left. Now Veranna found her voice, for her grip did not suffice against the force of the turn. Her heel slipped over the crest of Majestrin's back. She clawed the air.

Down she plummeted, and no word of prayer for Creo's rescue fought past her abject terror. How long would she fall before she collided with the merciless ground? Would she at least die instantly?

With gut-wrenching force, her fall jerked to a stop. This was no impact.

A rough surface pressed against her back and side, a sensation that demanded she make sense of her circumstances. Through one hesitantly opened eye, she discovered that Majestrin clutched her under one of his forelegs, curling her against his body.

"Should I...try to remount?" she asked.

"No." Majestrin's tone was brusque. "I should have assumed you had little hope of staying mounted. How many weeks has it taken me to teach Vinyanel such a skill, he who has remarkable talent for riding? No, Prophetess, I'd best carry you."

"It doesn't impede your flying?"

"I didn't say that. But I assume you should prefer it to riding inside my mouth."

Veranna shuddered. "This will suffice."

After a pause, Veranna bellowed over the wind. "Do we have a strategy? Surely the dragon-kin will now keep a keen eye for trouble."

"I am open to suggestions. I only hope I have been fast enough to intervene before..."

Majestrin's voice trailed off, though Veranna could not tell if he choked on the words or if his exertion merely stole them. She reached out with her spirit and sought the dragon's mood. He exuded veiled worry, a tremulous emotion chattering beneath a cool surface.

"You have grown attached to Vinyanel," Veranna said.

The dragon snorted. "Because his bristly exterior is just the most winsome thing."

Veranna found a chuckle in her heart. "Play it off if you will. Creo chose the right mount for him. The right prophetess? That still feels uncertain to me."

"Who can say for whose good the Maker has paired you?" Majestrin glided for a stretch. "None of it will matter if I tarry." With a groan, he heaved his wings into motion again.

"Let us hold to the hope that they will stay their hands, at least for a time." Veranna curled tighter against Majestrin. "I shall pray Creo's miraculous intervention."

"What will you ask of him?"

"It is very rarely a matter up to my choosing. We shall see how the Creator wishes to aid me, or better yet, both of us."

"Have you perfected any Virtusen applicable to a rescue from well-prepared warriors?" Majestrin asked.

"Creo has never used me as a combatant," Veranna said. "That's Vinyanel's realm."

"Then you have instructed him in the use of offensive magic?"

"Good heavens, no!" Veranna gaped. "Can you imagine him, at this stage of spiritual chaos, having magic to wrestle?"

Majestrin sighed. "I suppose that's true. May the Maker inspire you with solutions I have not yet been able to devise myself."

W as there a part of me left that did not roar in pain? I was thankful I no longer had any reflection nearby in which to see my battered visage. The only emotion that kept me from succumbing to despair was my raw fury over my captors' cowardice.

A warrior named Khagrosh asked the questions, a black-scaled counterpart dealt out the retribution for my unacceptable answers. Since I had produced no more satisfactory responses to their questions than the explanation that I had been flying alone / that night, on no mission from any superior, they had grown incensed. No matter what ribs they bruised or broke, how many fingers they dislocated, how many gauntlets I took across the face, my story remained unchanged.

"I'm going to ask you one more question, softbelly," Khagrosh said, his spittle spattering across my face as he leaned in. "What did your people do with the Chalice?"

I wanted to fling a belittlement about living in a society with divisions of labor, but my face simply hurt too much. "No...idea."

I took an armored knee to the groin that made me seriously question my future ability to father offspring.

"We are not so stupid as to think it is coincidence the worm who stole our artifact is the one to skulk around us yet again. Perhaps you wish to join your comrades, who Lord Scitherias's dread fury turned to ash?"

Once again, the mention of Scitherias's assault called to mind only a black space in my memory. A fluttering sense of panic began to tumble its way through my middle, joining the roiling misery remaining from the groin shot. I hung forward, against the bonds that secured me to the tent's center post.

"You have proven a nuisance one too many times, Captain," Khagrosh said. He turned to his black-scaled companion. "Tell his lordship this sack of sniveling swine excrement is only fit for the altar."

Well, that took them longer than I had expected.

The other dragon-kin snorted. "So quick to serve your priests."

They both turned to leave the tent.

Khagrosh growled. "Some of us ought to recall the gifts Quel-durik has granted us."

"While others ought not dismiss tactical advantages we might still wring from this softbelly's hide..."

Their conversation passed beyond hearing.

I could only guess what leverage Scitherias and the other creatures of military mind in his service thought they might glean from keeping me alive. Every moment the debate remained in play, however, was a moment I might use for my own purposes —namely, escape.

If only I might move without sending the world around me spinning. There was no denying it: I was a mess. Even so, I writhed against my bonds as I slumped down the pole. A fire's glow grew in the distance beyond the tent opening. Perhaps the debate was indeed dead, and my enemies now stoked flames that awaited my flesh to sate their demonic hunger.

A sharp intake of breath to my left drew my startled gaze, and I squinted my one eye that was not swollen shut to see what draconic creature had arrived to harry me further. But I saw nothing. Not that I trusted my vision at this point.

"Creo's mercy, Vinyanel! What have they done? I hardly recognize you."

The whispering voice belonged to Veranna, but nowhere did I see a half-elf to speak it. *Excellent.* Now hallucinations joined my list of maladies.

I groaned as another wave of nausea swept over me. I pressed my cheek to a crate beside me, knowing nothing remained in my stomach to vomit. Somehow, that still failed to make the heaving any easier.

"First things first, Captain," Veranna's voice went on, despite my efforts to disbelieve it and push it from my mind. A whispering chant full of archaic words from the ancient history of my people drifted through the air, reminding me of the rocking flight of a feather as it settles to earth. Like cold water down a parched throat, a subtle pressure that began in my chest rippled through my body. My pain ebbed. My nausea lessened.

A sigh. "Well, I suppose that is all the Creator sees fit to grant."

"I must be dying," I muttered. "I hear you forget your agony when the end nears."

"Vinyanel, you ninny!" the Veranna-voice blurted. "I'm here."

Just when I thought my circumstances could grow no worse. A groan rumbled from my throat.

"You can thank me for coming later. Can you get up?" Veranna said.

"Does it look like I can?" I resisted the urge to tack *you ninny* onto my reply. My split lips made each successive word more agonizing to form, to Veranna's good fortune. "Do you have a plan?"

"Majestrin is timing a distraction."

My hands slipped free of my bonds as I heard the unmistakable *snick* of a knife through hemp.

I ground my teeth. "It sounds less than foolproof, but if that is all—"

"Going batty, softbelly?" a gruff voice croaked at me as the black-scaled dragon-kin threw open the tent flap. "Whimpering to yourself won't make this any better for you. Looks like it's time for the roast."

Now that I saw him better, with my less-swollen eyes and significantly clearer vision, I got a good look at the reptilian sadist who had been my interrogator. Many of his scales bore the deep clefts of old wounds, long scarred shut. One of his eyes, obscured under a milky film, roved independently of the other. The teeth that protruded from his dramatic underbite smelled of decay, even from a distance.

He grabbed me by my fouled tunic and pulled me to my feet. In a last-minute flash of lucidity, I laced my fingers together to keep my hands behind the pole. His eyes narrowed as he flicked his tongue. "Either you're some kind of fast healer, or something slippery is afoot."

A leathery shaft pressed against my knuckles. I knew the grip of a sword when I felt it.

Not a good idea.

Clearly, Veranna had less of a plan than I feared. I dared not let the sword clatter from my hand, so my other option was to use it, however ill-advised that might be. My only hope stood in killing this creature in one stroke. A failed attempt would do nothing but raise alarm. I gripped the hilt.

"So, is it my job to uproot this pole and haul it with me to the altar?" I slurred. "I do not know that I have the strength, as thorough as you have been in your interrogation."

A dark smile crept across the dragon-kin's face. "You've got quite the sense of humor for one in your position." He bent down and grasped the bonds around my ankles, a blade of blood-colored steel in his other hand.

The sword I held whistled as I swept it around. I plunged it between his shoulder blades with practiced precision, and the interrogator immediately slumped at my feet.

"Excellent work, Captain!" Veranna said. "In a horrible sort of way."

My breath lodged in my throat as she spoke full-voice, for just as the words emerged, three more dragon-kin marched into the tent. Here I stood, feet still bound, holding the hilt of a sword that stuck in one of my captors' backs, with Veranna's disembodied feminine voice hanging in the air.

The only creature who drew my focus was the central dragon-kin, his black and red robe and large gargoyle talisman around his neck announcing his role of priest. The look of boiling fury on his face twisted his already grotesque features to horrific disfigurement. He croaked something in his own language and threw his hand out in front of him in a sweeping arc. Smoky ripples the color of old blood curled from his hand and flooded the space around me.

In my peripheral vision, a crouching Veranna appeared, a

bare-bladed dagger gleaming in her white-knuckled grip. The priest's smoke tendrils dissipated.

"I don't suppose this was all part of the plan?" I said through my teeth.

She sawed her blade through the bonds on my ankles, but not soon enough. One of the dragon-kin who had accompanied the priest lunged at Veranna, while another charged me.

My assailant slammed his shoulder into my chest and slammed me back into the post before I wrenched the sword free of my victim. The force of the impact buffeted the breath from my lungs and awoke explosions of pain across my already-damaged ribs. My torso spasmed for want of air.

Veranna's attacker grappled her and twisted the weapon from her hand. She yelped in pain. He pinned her to the tent floor with a knee planted on her spine.

The priest folded his arms and chuckled. "Looks like Quel-durik shall be doubly pleased with our offering tonight."

9

DETERMINATION'S FLAME

"To the abyss with your sham-god Queldurik!" My lack of breath undermined my voice, but hatred contorted my features. I thrust the dragon-kin's weight off me and lunged for the sword. After a feint left, I swung for the dragon-kin priest before me. His yelp told me he had not anticipated such boldness—or was it stupidity—on my part. My blade bit into his chest, and he staggered back, clutching the long wound and snarling. A flurry of gravely words spilled from his lips.

The creature who I had thrown aside snatched Veranna's knife from the floor and dove at me. Were I more callous to the horrors of war, I would have found his feeble opposition laughable. Finally, with my limbs free and a real weapon in hand, they would discover with whom they dealt. He fell upon a grimly efficient upward thrust from my blade.

A throaty note cut through the air. Veranna's captor had placed a curving black horn to his lips, and the sound drove slivers of panic into my gut. To my left, a flicker of unwholesome, greenish light gleamed: otherworldly energy pulsed across the priest's wound as he enacted the dark magic that would knit his flesh back together. I vacillated for a moment. Kill Veranna's captor, finish the priest, or prepare for the inevitable onslaught the horn would draw?

The scaly warriors that bounded through the tent opening made my next decision for me. My longsword flashed in arcs of devastation and rid the world of four more abominations before the sheer press of numbers overwhelmed me. It took one dragon-kin soldier for each of my limbs, but they succeeded in dragging me back to the ground. My face crashed against the hard clay, rattling my teeth.

What had Veranna been doing all this time? Was there no Virtus of Creo she might have called upon to, at the very least, ensure her own escape? I suspected her power in Creo had confronted little practical testing in the face of crisis.

My captors dragged me across the camp while I thrashed and cursed them in Elvish. They slammed my back against a thick stake, and when they lashed me to it, they made sure not to skimp on the amount of rope they wound around me. Splinters from the hewn post bit into my back.

I stood in full view of a grisly sacrifice altar, which rose upon a platform of stone blocks. At its pinnacle stood a hauntingly stark figure: a cast iron shape of a featureless man, his arms outstretched before him and his surface scorched with many passages in and out of flame. A dozen braziers that ringed the profane place smoked and crackled, and heaps of fuel beneath the idol awaited their charge. Why they stopped short of hauling me up the dais right away, I did not understand, but I accepted this small measure of mercy without hesitation.

The dragon-kin tightened the last rope until it cut into my arms, but an unmistakable shriek demanded my focus. A pair of enemy warriors dragged Veranna to the altar as well. Her convulsive struggling made no difference. They bore her up the stairs and thrust her into the arms of the idol, clamping shackles upon her ankles and arms that secured her in the iron embrace of death. Her scream of resistance transformed to an undeniable keen of agony.

Fury like none I had ever experienced roared through my flesh, raising beads of sweat on my back and brow. Stand and watch as they put the prophetess to flame? No matter my personal quibbles with her, I would not permit such an offense. Of course, what I could do about it remained elusive.

I strained against my bonds, but moved a scant few inches. Creo's healing had given me some strength, but I felt half the elf I might have been that night. I wrestled to clear the fog from my mind to generate some workable tactics, if indeed any existed.

The fury of darkness has no bite where Creo's faithful oppose it.

I blinked against the unbidden memory of words I had read weeks prior.

The dragon-kin priest strode up to Veranna as she lay across the idol's outstretched arms, writhing in her shackles, eyes closed, lips moving. From beneath his hood, his voice boomed in a ceremonious lilt. The creatures that ringed the altar lifted their hands, the orange light of torches and braziers dancing in their eyes, reflecting dully off their scales. They intoned as one. Again, I understood nothing but the constant repetition of the name *Queldurik*. Through the blurring air created by the heat of flames, the crowd weaved in a grotesque dance of dark appetite.

The priest lifted a torch to one of the braziers, lit it, and carried it to the wood and tinder beneath Veranna with purposeful, reverent steps. I thrashed against my bonds, sure I would break my body if not the ropes. A surge of—something—like a lightning storm contained in my skin rushed through me.

"*Though they commit my servants to the ash heap, how they will wail when destruction forsakes them.*" This time, the continuation of words from *The Tree* passed my lips. Distress must have been breaking my mind.

The priest lowered the flame.

He waited.

The tinder did not so much as smoke, let alone catch.

He lashed his tail, perturbed, and croaked to the creatures around him. A few scuttled to the pyre, flinging oil upon the wood...even on Veranna herself.

Still, no flame caught upon fuel or half-elf.

"A blight upon you, elf-witch!" The priest threw his torch to the ground. "You will burn, if not alive, in pieces!" He pulled a knife with a long, curved blade from a sheath on his hip, its blade ablaze from the brazier light around it.

I thrashed again, and the cords around my chest went slack.

A sudden roar shook both the air and the earth with its potency. From above, from no source I could see, came a massive column of white, steaming liquid, a column that pummeled the crowd of dragon-kin around the altar. Every creature it engulfed turned to ice, frozen in whatever pose of terror they took as the attack overwhelmed them.

Majestrin? Though I saw no dragon in the flesh, the products of his assault proclaimed his arrival.

All the while, Veranna remained in the idol's arms, mouthing words beyond my hearing, but it mattered little, for the dragon-kin scattered before Majestrin's attack like leaves before the wind. I strained once more against my bonds, and the last of the ropes fell away. Even the fetters on my hands and ankles fell limp to the ground. But why?

I would contemplate it later. For now, I leapt away from my post, bounding up the stairs in three steps. The dragon-kin priest had fled the place and was now scrambling among his kinsmen, bellowing orders.

I pried apart Veranna's shackles. To my horror, the insides of the iron cuffs bore rows of spikes like shark's teeth, and the restraints were sticky with her blood. Even the platform where I stood wore the crimson stain of her wounds. Without a thought, I lifted Veranna from her prison.

"Can you stand?"

"I...I think so." Veranna swayed on her feet, but stayed upright. "Praise the Maker! He freed you! He hears my prayers!"

I would have pondered the prophetess's words more closely had some of the dragon-kin not gathered their wits and realized their sacrifices were escaping. Six of their warriors ascended the platform stairs, weapons drawn. I glanced about in desperation.

Veranna's voice broke into a musical chant as I flung myself at one of the braziers. I gripped the anchored pole. The shaft grated and twisted, and with a final heave, slid free of its place on the dais.

The prophetess thrust her hands toward the dragon-kin, and a cloud of lavender mist swirled forth. The front three attackers' eyes rolled. They slumped to the ground. I leapt past Veranna, brandishing the brazier. A whirlwind of blows with my improvised polearm finished the remaining warriors before they reached the prophetess.

Never, ever, would I so much as leave my bed without a sword in hand again.

I pulled a longsword and a morningstar off the warriors we downed and swirled them with a bravado that dared another of their foul kind to try the stairs. *Crunch. Slash.* Two more abominations met their end under the swift assault I waged upon them, though most of the enemies backpedaled, their eyes bulging as they scanned the skies. How long had it been since Majestrin last breathed his worst upon them? The dark, vengeful part of me anticipated his next volley of annihilation.

The activity amidst the chaos that worried me most was the priest's, even though a legion of dragon-kin stood between him and me. He bellowed the same set of words, again and again, flinging his hand in an arc across the sky. Every time, curling blood-smoke followed in the path of his gesture. After his fifth attempt, Majestrin winked into view, no more than twenty paces away. Majestrin descended upon his prey.

The last, terrifying vision the priest beheld: Majestrin's wide maw.

The dragon clamped bone-crushing fangs upon the priest. With a flick of his head, he hurled the villain in a high arc, which to my relief, carried my adversary so far from the dais that I scarcely heard the sickening thud when his body landed.

Majestrin snatched both Veranna and me from the platform. We sped into the air. A cacophony of croaks and shouts erupted from the dragon-kin below, and the warriors among them scrambled to take aim with the stout bows of their kind. Arrows flew in a whistling storm, many of them glancing from Majestrin's silver hide, but a few either pricking or sticking fast. One dart grazed my leg. Veranna, curled in a very tight ball against Majestrin's body, avoided the volley. The dragon bolted skyward, quickly moving out of bowshot, but the ascent reawakened my stomach woes in an instant.

I gulped the lump in my throat. "Excellent timing, my friend!" I bellowed over the wind.

"It took the two of you long enough to get loose!" Majestrin replied. "That release, capture, release business made my part of the strategy nebulous, at best."

I grunted. "Patrons ablaze, that mess was a strategy? I venture that nothing short of a miracle got us out of there."

"Finally, Captain, you give credit where it is due!" Veranna interjected, though her words slurred together.

While I was hardly in the mood for tutoring, I could not deny the verity of her words. We had needed far more than my strength or skill to avoid a gruesome end, and war had taught me that battles rarely brought with them multiple strokes of luck. The clash of curses and Creo's power left my mind abuzz with questions peppered with awe.

"Can you ride, Vinyanel?" Majestrin called back to me. "We shall make better time back to Delsinon if I have you astride rather than having to lug you like a sack of turnips."

"I can manage it." I swallowed my worries that my dizziness might prove a fetter if the dragon-kin embattled us in the air. Sack of turnips, indeed.

I glanced behind me at the ever-shrinking flicker of firelight at the center of the dragon-kin camp. I discovered no signs of pursuit.

Majestrin plucked me from beneath his foreleg and craned his neck around to place me astride his back. Just as deftly, he slipped Veranna into both of his front talons and clutched her against his underside. The fact that she did not shriek surprised me.

I peered over Majestrin's shoulder to seek Veranna's newfound source of confidence. However, a brave countenance I did not find, but rather the rolling eyes and limp limbs of one semi-conscious.

"We do need to hasten home, Majestrin. But we shan't fly a course to Delsinon yet. Seek the cover of the mountains. I do not see any dragon-kin, but—"

"Oh, at least a few follow. I would know that stench from miles distant," Majestrin said.

We wheeled to the northeast, aiming for the craggy southern arm of the Triastead Mountains. When we reached their foothills, I told Majestrin to fly a low and winding course. Only if we confounded our pursuers might I hope to stabilize the situation.

10

PRIORITIES

EVEN THE GLORIOUS, golden light of the dawn could not brighten Veranna's sickly pallor. When Majestrin set her down amidst the rocks of the Southern Triastead Mountains, her legs gave way, and he had to lay her down instead. I crept toward her, bearing the waterskin I had filled at a nearby spring. She did not lift her head from the stony ground. Her quickened breaths and the dew of sweat that beaded upon her brow corroborated her peril.

I knelt beside her to survey her condition. I breathed through my teeth in a steady rhythm in hopes of regulating my own pain. Pools of red soaked the bandages I had clumsily applied to her wrists and shins during a brief rest from flight. The dragon-kin might not have succeeded in sacrificing her as they intended, but her weakness made me wonder if I had only temporarily forestalled her doom. While an elf of warrior's mettle might have borne the hurts with better fortitude, she was no warrior, in the traditional sense.

"Can you drink, Prophetess?"

She opened her eyes, though pain clouded them. In response to her mute nod, I tipped the skin to her lips. Her swallows required visible effort.

"Thank you, Captain." Her dry voice crackled in her throat like stiff paper.

Majestrin ambled closer to us. "What now, Vinyanel? The dragon-kin stench is gone, and has been for several hours, so we have at least outrun them for now. With luck, we've lost them."

"I should, first and foremost, like to know what that encampment was doing on elven soil. If they have been here long enough to build an altar, we have surely grown blind." I stood to pace the gully in which we rested—or rather to limp, given the arrow that had scored my thigh during our escape. My lingering vertigo, throbbing head, cuts, bruises, and body aches threatened my balance, but I stubbornly fought the detestable heralds of frailty.

"Perhaps they seek retribution over the Chalice. Or is there some other aggression they might perpetrate on your kind?" Majestrin asked.

"Their efforts are futile, whatever their goal," I said. "For centuries, the illusions have protected our capital city from discovery. They have no hope of launching an offensive."

"Do not lean overmuch on the accomplishments of the past, young Windrider," Veranna said, albeit in a whisper. "The dragon-kin are tenacious and have shown us they will sacrifice as many of their own as it takes to accomplish their ends. Perhaps they failed to detain us, but who knows what intricacies may be at work." By the time she finished speaking, she gasped for air as one on a long run.

It set my teeth on edge. Something about the way that phrase, "young Windrider," rolled from her tongue never made it sound like a compliment. I hardly heard the rest of what she said beyond it. Her lecture uprooted any shoots of sympathy that might have sprouted in my soul over her condition.

"Whatever their aim, they have overreached, daring to make camp within striking distance of Delsinon's army. We must report back. Swift action will show these vile aberrations that no quarter will be allowed to them."

Majestrin turned a weary gaze to me. "I have done nothing but fly for the past twelve hours, and most of that at top speed."

I sighed. "I understand. How long must you rest before we make the flight home?"

"I shall need at least a few hours' rest before the journey will be safe for us all."

I wanted to crack my knuckles, but the dull throb in my black-and-blue fingers reminded me Creo's healing had not fully repaired the damage my interrogator had inflicted upon my hands. In fact, the longer we remained idle in that gully, the more profoundly I noticed the wages of my time spent in the dragon-kin's company. Scarcely had I healed the wounds acquired in the winning of the Chalice just a few weeks prior, and now I had a fresh batch to try to ignore. The reality drew my eye again to Veranna.

I wondered how much blood she had truly lost. While she drowsed, I crept over to her leather satchel of provisions. She could forgive me later for rifling through her equipment.

I pulled what remained of the bindings and balms she brought, supplies she doubtless thought she might need for me. With the provisions tucked under my arm, I knelt beside her.

"We had best change your dressings, Prophetess."

She made no more response than to tense her muscles against the inevitable discomfort. When I gingerly drew back the crusty bandage, her eyes snapped open, and she drew a hissing breath. The punctures in her flesh were deep. If she weathered the blood loss, infection would be the next enemy she faced.

I worked in silence for a time, before Veranna mustered the composure to speak. "I am so thankful for the Virtus that released you from your bonds. I do not know how else we might have escaped."

I raised an eyebrow at her. "Virtus? Is it not more likely owing to a faulty knot?"

"Every word of the prayers I uttered while on that altar was for your release. Surely you do not think so much of your own strength that you believe you overcame the bonds of your own accord?"

A flush rose in my cheeks. I re-rolled the remaining bandages. "Well, I..."

Veranna shook her head. "I saw the knots, and they were substantial."

I paused in my work. "You mean to say you prayed not for your own preservation in the face of the flames? Then how is it the fuel would not light?"

"The Creator has granted me no revelation to that end." Veranna closed her eyes again.

I moved on to re-bind Veranna's shins. Had our places been reversed, would I have thought first of her escape? Were the words from *The Tree* the outpouring of my own soul, or the Maker's reminder of my own inadequacy?

"It grows clear to me that..." The words stuck in my throat. They would not defeat me, however. There was power in their admission. "I need to cultivate in my own spirit your priority for others."

"You forget, Vinyanel," said Majestrin, his drowsy voice rumbling from nearby, "you have already shown some of that quality. You placed yourself between the dragon-kin and me. Insisted upon my survival by dismissing me in the ambush in the clearing."

That much was true. I had put Majestrin's survival ahead of my own, but that was easy to do. I admired him. He was magnificent. Did I have the strength of character to make the same sacrifice for those who garnered none of my affection? Surely, my eventual role as commander would demand that.

"Fret not." Majestrin curled into a ball on the stony ground. "Creo is strong enough to mold you into what he wants you to be, if you will let him."

I did not question the plausibility of Majestrin's words—only my strength to withstand the vigorous refining process it would take to...I pushed the thought down. I stood and took a few steps from my comrades. "Rest then, both of you. When you have gathered some strength, we shall make our way home."

When Majestrin landed at the drawbridge of Delsinon's fortress, I made no apologies to any of the perfumed courtiers around us about the batteredness of my condition, but instead shouldered straight through them, carrying the still-weak prophetess in my arms.

As we crossed to the gate, the soldier standing guard there clenched his fist over his heart and bowed to me. "Captain. What business shall I enter in the ledger for your passage of the gate today?"

The formality of the protocol chafed me. "I seek audience with Chancellor Lerendir. He is about, correct?"

"I believe so, Captain." He cast a doubtful glance upon me, then Veranna. "Are you sure you would not first wish a stop at the infirmary?"

"I have no time for coddling," I said. "Good morning."

I swept past the guard, leaving him to scribble whatever he would into the ledger. As we crossed the outer bailey, a figure jogged up next to me. I exhaled audibly. It would take me until luncheon to reach the Chancellor's chambers if someone apprehended me every dozen steps. I turned a steely gaze to the approaching elf.

My glare fell upon the six-pointed star insignia on the soldier's black waistcoat, so I choked back my tirade. Rather, I brought my feet together and performed as effective a bow I could, carrying a half-elf as I was.

"Major."

The degree of shock and pity on the major's face took me

by surprise. "Veranna?" He placed his hand upon her wan cheek. "Thank the Maker you have made it back! My detachment and I were on the brink of marching in search for you." He glanced up at me. "For both of you, of course. What happened?"

"With all due respect, Major, I would rather not brief every elf I pass. I seek Chancellor Lerendir on matters urgent to our security."

"Good enough, Captain. But I must ask," the major said, "is this something Veranna must attend? She looks—how to put it?" He rubbed the back of his neck. "Unwell."

I paused to consider it. "I suppose not. I have learned much of her perspective on the events, which I can relay well enough."

The major reached to take her from my arms. "Then I shall see to her care."

Veranna's eyes opened slowly, and she looked up into the major's face.

"Galdurith." Veranna smiled.

The creased expression of sympathy that overtook the major's face convinced me to deposit Veranna in his care. Better him than me, that was clear. I eased Veranna into his arms.

"Good luck." I straightened my tattered tunic, then marched to the keep with a quickened, if limping, step.

"Just how large a unit of these villains squats within our borders, then?" Chancellor Lerendir poured a goblet of deep garnet wine and offered it to me.

I waved the goblet off. The effects of alcohol would only worsen my already questionable sense of balance. "Majestrin estimated at least five hundred, Chancellor. Too small a group to consider any kind of serious aggression, but too large to scatter without a significant fight."

"At the very least, it seems you've agitated them with your last campaign." Lerendir sipped the wine.

Even if the Chancellor's assessment proved true, I could not fathom what maneuver the dragon-kin staged with their limited resources.

"I recommended to Majestrin that we take a pass or two more and eliminate a few score, but he would have nothing of it."

The Chancellor chuckled, the first soft look I had seen cross his face that morning. "No? Just who is the soldier and who the mount, Captain?"

I straightened in my seat. "The situation differs—"

"Relax, Captain, I know. You are ceaselessly intense, and I find it exhausting to watch." He took a sip of the wine. "While I am loath to waste the time in trying it, we must first take the path of diplomacy."

"If I were you, I should send a few regiments of cavalry and no shortage of foot soldiers just behind the ambassador."

"No doubt. Is Sergeant Althoron capable of managing your detachment in your absence?"

"My absence?" I furrowed my brow, even though it aggravated my headache. "I have complete confidence in his capabilities, but why should his performance be tested?"

"Have you looked in a glass, Captain?" The Chancellor smirked. "You are wounded, and none of your denying it will convince me otherwise. Judging by the look of your eyes alone, I believe you to be concussed, and I shan't send you afield in that state. Too much rides on you."

"So you place me in the hands of a nursemaid until you decide on a time for my unveiling?" I jumped to my feet, though I also made a quick grab for the arm of my chair as the room once again whirled.

Chancellor Lerendir ducked his chin in a single nod. "Don't worry, Captain Ecleriast. I plan on offering you plenty of opportunities to get yourself killed in the future." He clapped me on the shoulder. "For now, your assignment is the infirmary."

I opened my mouth for further protest, but the Chancellor's smile turned stern.

"Do not make me say it, Captain."

"Yes, sir. I see this is not a suggestion, but an order."

I shuffled to the infirmary, willfully offering no facial response to the elves I passed, comrades who gaped with astonished stares. The dragon-kin must have made quite a dent in my appearance. As I stepped through the white doors of the wing, a pair of yellow-robed elves greeted me.

"We have been expecting you, Captain." One of the healers squinted at me. "You may be here longer than Veranna guessed."

I peered past the pair of healers and found the prophetess propped on a pillow on a nearby cot. Though still pale, she looked comfortable and well-tended. Her drowsy gaze fell upon me, and she patted a copy of *The Tree* that lay in her lap.

"Welcome, Vinyanel. Looks like we shall have a few days' uninterrupted time to catch up on some of this studying you have neglected."

"Days?" My glance vaulted from Veranna to the healers nearby.

They nodded to one another.

I threw my hands out toward Veranna. "Now that you are tended, I need to find Emynon and hear what he has—"

Each of the two infirmary attendants took me by an arm.

"You'll be lucky if we let you do anything so strenuous as having the prophetess read to you," one of them said.

"I have read the book, every word," I said.

"Reading is not studying," Veranna replied.

I suppressed a groan. A pity my injuries were not worse. A bout of unconsciousness would have been bliss about then.

——————

"Vinyanel, are you listening to me at all?"

My eyes snapped open and I shook my head. "Yes, of course, Prophetess."

Veranna stared at me with her arms folded and her lips pursed.

"All right, no." I leaned back on my hands and adjusted my seated position on my infirmary cot.

To be fair, it was not entirely Veranna's fault I dozed off while she taught. The very atmosphere of the infirmary—stiflingly quiet, changeless, whether day or night—contributed to my existing insomnia. Left to my own devices, I would have been riding or training to beat back the waves of drowsiness that always overtook me in the afternoon.

"There's so much to cover," she said. "Can you please try, at least a little, to stay with me?"

I rubbed my face with my palms. "All right. I will try harder. This last week of forced convalescence is absolutely counter—"

The door at the far end of the infirmary rows of beds swung open with a low groan of hinges. Two white-tabarded pages who carried banners of the royal scroll-and-sword livery flanked the entry. Through them strode King Saransaeloth, followed closely by his new champion, clad in buckskin leather armor and a plum three-quarter length cape. The fact that he followed the king unsupervised rumored the Blackwatch had learned nothing concerning him. Yet.

I rose and spun to face them. The full bow of salute I performed elicited protest from my ribs and a head rush, but at least I had recovered sufficiently to mask the discomforts.

"At ease, Captain," Saransaeloth said.

I straightened. "To what do I owe the honor of your presence, my lord?"

Mithveranon waited silently three paces back from the king, his glance roving the surroundings. He carried a lithe sabre at his side, but despite the weapon's smaller size, he still stood too close to His Majesty.

The king glanced over his shoulder, then connected gazes with me. "What are you frowning at, Captain?"

Warmth rose in my cheeks. I cleared my throat. "My apologies, sire." I rolled my lips in and fought to reset my expression.

Veranna stepped to my side. "Do forgive my student, Your Majesty. Healing doesn't sit well with his obsessive—"

Saransaeloth raised a palm, and Veranna bit off her statement.

"No, I implore you, Captain. What have you found to your disliking?"

Well, he asked.

"Your champion is standing too close to you to be able to properly draw a bladed weapon of the size he carries and defend you in this space, should the need arise."

A light smirk appeared on Saransaeloth's lips. I deliberately dodged Mithveranon's glance.

"Aha, so I am right to come to you in this matter," the king said. "Mithveranon needs training in his office. Being born and raised in our seaside holdings, not here in Delsinon, he lacks a certain depth of understanding about how we conduct ourselves."

A surge of prickling energy ran through my limbs. Finally, a reason to escape this smothering nest of quietude.

"With all due respect, Your Majesty," Veranna said, "Vinyanel sustained heavy injuries last week, and has just now begun to make progress in his study with me. Cannot last year's champion perform this duty?"

"Frankly, Veranna, he cannot." The king leveled a stern gaze at her. "He has taken very ill, and those I trust with this task are few in number. Vinyanel has a long set of years ahead of him in which he must learn to balance his spiritual and earthly duties. Let this be an early lesson."

I ducked my chin. "It would be my privilege to serve you in this way, my lord."

Veranna propped her hand on her hip. "You're going to be a busy mentor-student then, Vinyanel. I will not be ignored over this new assignment that speaks more to your tastes."

I lifted a brow. "So much for 'Vinyanel sustained heavy injuries last week.'"

"You're impossible." Veranna plunked onto her cot and slapped her copy of *The Tree* shut. "Your Majesty? When do you deem it acceptable that the captain turn his attentions to his calling?"

Saransaeloth smirked. "After sunset, Prophetess, he's all yours."

"As His Majesty's personal guard as well as champion, you will find you need to cooperate often with our intelligence here in the city, the Blackwatch," I told Mithveranon as we passed along the corridor outside Saransaeloth's chambers of meeting.

"Ah, yes," Mithveranon said. "I've already exchanged no few words with them, over that unfortunate situation regarding the poor fellow they found who was deemed to look like me."

"*They* found?" I screwed a brow down.

"Had you not heard?" Mithveranon said. "Oh, perfect, now I've done it."

I chuckled, but not with mirth. "Not to worry. I have certainly heard."

Emynon's investigation must have stalled in dead ends if they resorted to simply spilling the story of the corpse to their prime person of interest.

After a pause to look out over the inner bailey from the tall window beside me, I continued. "For the most part, they will keep you apprised to any concerns they have during large assemblies here in the fortress, or when the king's presence is required in the city. You are the last line of defense should any perimeter they set fail."

"This perimeter," Mithveranon said. "Do they keep it at all times?"

"Yes and no..." I fixed upon Mithveranon's gray eyes. The king had brought the young champion to me for education—surely that included details about the royal guard and their duties. The champion's eyes remained locked upon mine, wide and earnest. But still, the unresolved mystery of the corpse left me ill at ease. "Your best policy is to assume you are the only elf standing between the king and an assassin, no matter the circumstances. If you seek further specifics on the Blackwatch's role in this, perhaps implore of His Majesty to assign one of them to your training as well."

Mithveranon sighed. "Very well." He laughed. "Believe it or not, you're the easier soldier to work with."

I tilted my head. These words were certainly ones I had never heard applied to me even once during my six decades of service. "You clearly do not know me very well yet."

We reached the junction of the meeting corridor and the Royal Chambers wing. I turned to pace back the way we had come.

"What are the bronze doors in this hallway, Captain?" Mithveranon peered around the corner.

I glanced back over my shoulder. "Oh. The treasury. Not technically your responsibility."

"Where they keep the royal family's personal assets?"

"Not as I understand it." I frowned. "Contents of sensitive

areas are typically only discussed on a need-to-know basis. I have never been one who needs to know."

Mithveranon tightened his white-blonde ponytail. "Just working to piece together what sorts of ruffians would have any interest in this area, you understand."

I spent the remainder of the king's meetings drilling Mithveranon on close combat techniques and, as I had guessed from his positioning in the infirmary, he lacked practical knowledge in this area. He moved with uncanny speed and strength. His sabre technique was excellent, as the tournament had proven, but his instincts on how to manage swordplay somewhere besides the contest ring were green.

It would be a lie to say I did not get a bit of sick pleasure out of jumping from shadowed niches and watching him scramble.

After the fourth instance in which I laid my blade across his throat, the approach of jingling footfalls tarnished my amusement. The sky beyond the castle windows still blushed with a rose sunset when Veranna appeared around the corner. Her eyes widened when she spotted us.

I released Mithveranon.

He straightened his tabard and laughed. "Nursemaid come to fetch you to supper?"

He was cheeky for a soldier who I had theoretically bested a half-dozen times in the last quarter-hour.

I rolled my eyes. "I am not even late yet, Veranna."

"You've set a precedent, Captain." Her glance flicked to Mithveranon, and a light shudder passed over the prophetess.

I cast her a quizzical look.

"It's chilly in this wing," she said.

"Probably the northward-facing windows." Mithveranon unclasped his cloak. "Might I offer my mantle? My pants?" He smirked.

Veranna regarded him with a flat gaze. "You should remain in full uniform, as I understand it."

He shrugged and donned the garment again. "All the cheer of a mausoleum, keeping company with the two of you!"

We descended the stairs to the main entry to the royal wing, where I conveyed Mithveranon into the keeping of the Blackwatch detachment of the king's guard for the evening.

"Work on your close-quarters technique!" I called as Veranna towed me away by my arm.

Once we had left the fortress proper to cross the inner ward for the chapel, Veranna released my arm. "Mithveranon gives me the shivers."

"He has a bit of a wolfish air, I suppose."

"Indeed. Something about his eyes—hungry and...I don't know."

I shrugged. "The look of a competitor."

"It's different, Captain," she said. "You have the hard edge of a competitor in your eyes, but Mithveranon is different. Feral."

"And yet he retains his access to His Majesty and the inner keep."

Veranna turned to face me and placed both her hands on my shoulders. "The more I encounter him, the more I am glad you are assigned some of his training. Be vigilant."

I blinked. At least someone agreed with me that perhaps more remained undiscovered about the mysterious dead twin of the king's champion, although I had not expected to find that common ground with Veranna.

"You can count on that, Prophetess."

11

MURKY TERMS

AFTER THREE HOURS OF STUDY, cross-referencing, and slogging through Virtusen theory in Veranna's keeping, I shuffled my way back to my quarters. Long yawns plagued me all the way across the fortress grounds, and muscles stiff from disuse protested my every stride. Perhaps I had overdone it—just a touch—in drilling Mithveranon.

I pushed open the door to my quarters. Inside, moonlight filtered through the window over my bunk, the coverlet as smooth as I had left it what seemed like ages ago. My dress, field, and paddock boots stood tidily at the foot of the bed. My suit of field plate covered the mannequin just beyond, its rents and scars tended but still imperfect. I took a deep breath. Finally, I returned to my only true place of solitude.

I turned and shut the door softly, but the hair on the back of my neck stood on end. My hand flew to my sword belt.

"Shh, shh, it's just me." Mithveranon stepped from the corner my door had blocked. He held empty hands at shoulder height.

My heart thumped against my ribs, but I drew a breath through my nostrils and relaxed my grip. "What are you doing here?"

He put his fingers to his lips. "Not so loud. I don't have a lot of time, so listen carefully."

I folded my arms across my chest. "This had better be important for you to be out of the keep at this hour." *Unattended.* I contained the thought behind my teeth.

"I heard something on rounds tonight that I thought you'd better know about."

I waited. A skeptical frown pulled at my lip.

"That encampment you found...of the...what are they called?" Mithveranon said.

"Dragon-kin?"

"Yes! The Blackwatch have word those creatures keep a member of your unit prisoner," Mithveranon continued. "One from the mission north where you came back with Veranna and the dragon."

The statement punched me in the chest. "What?" Alarms clanged in the back of my mind. "Why are you telling me this?"

Mithveranon lowered his voice further. "The Blackwatch are planning on rejecting an offer of negotiations from the dragon-kin."

"This is sensitive information, Mithveranon," I said. "Maybe that means little to you in your experience, but you realize you risk your new station by retelling what you heard."

"I know." Mithveranon looked at the floor. "But it's not right that the higher officers should throw away a soldier's life, is it? I have every reason to believe Major Emynon already knew about the prisoner—Curunith, is it—when he allowed Veranna to fly to the encampment."

Words failed me. I laced my fingers behind my neck and paced.

"What does Emynon have against you, anyway?"

A sardonic laugh escaped me. "Damned if I know. The only reasons I can see are either completely unprofessional or fantastically immature."

Sweat beaded on my brow. I paced a couple more passes of the small room. The temple bells tolled in the distance.

"We are set to reconvene at the third hour after rising, correct?" I stared out my window. Only under optimal circumstances would I get back in time to appear as assigned. One did not fail to appear for a royally appointed duty.

"Do...you want my help?" Mithveranon said. "I mean, such as it is."

I furrowed my brow at him.

"Look, you might not be very likable, Captain, but I do respect you, after having worked with you." Mithveranon clasped his hands behind his back.

The temple bells fell silent after ten mournful peals.

I shook my head and stepped over to my armor to lift the breastplate from the mannequin. "No. The offer is a noble one, but no." If I was planning on destroying anyone's future in the king's service, it should only be my own.

"Didn't you take enough of a beating the first time?" Majestrin said. He lowered his head back to the moon-dappled forest floor.

"I appreciate your confidence in me." I adjusted the buckles on my frog to better angle my scabbard for riding. "You know I cannot just leave this to an impassive rejection of terms."

"I also know you have absolutely no plan."

I blew out a breath. "In the worst-case scenario, I will only be able to gather information on where they are holding Curunith, and then we can return for his release—during daylight hours when the dragon-kin will be subject to the sun sickness."

"Won't that interfere with your assignments?" Majestrin asked.

"I will find a way to make arrangements." I shouldered my pack.

"Why not simply broach the subject with one of the Blackwatch commanders? They may have intelligence to help you."

"Fabulous idea. Come to their commanders with information to which I am not privy, then ask them to tell me the rest so I can take over their situation. High likelihood of success."

"Worse than flying in solo?" Majestrin tilted his head.

"What I do with my repose time is of my own choosing." I glanced back at what twinkling lights along Delsinon's outer wall peeked between trunks and branches. "If I start nosing around in Emynon's business, I doubt he will hesitate to see that ends in an inquest, if not shackles."

Majestrin huffed a thin cloud of frosty swirls. "You people and your pride."

"I do not know what the dragon-kin ask in exchange for Curunith, but if it is true that my people are not entertaining negotiations, do you not see that I cannot just leave him?" I said. "He bought my life. Our mission would have likely failed utterly, were it not for his self-sacrifice."

"He did a soldier's duty," Majestrin said.

"But I do not pursue him as a soldier." I turned my back on Majestrin. "I go as a friend."

Majestrin shuffled his wings. He stretched his neck around me and looked me in the eye. "I will take you where you want to go, but I make no secret of the fact that I have a bad feeling about it."

"I will lead as wisely as I know how, I promise." I placed a foot on the upper section of Majestrin's wing, and he boosted me to his back.

We charged a few strides through the forest until Majestrin reached a clearing at the north end of Lake Nuinna. With a few mighty thrusts of his wings, we left earth and water behind for the exhilarating embrace of the open sky. The silver of both dragon and moonlight glinted from the surface of the lake as we ascended. Perhaps now there were two places where I could truly feel in accord with myself.

"Keep your nose to the wind, my friend," I said.

"I fully intend to," Majestrin answered. "If I scent more than a distant tingle out of place, we adjust our plans."

While we flew, I reviewed in my mind what little of the dragon-kin encampment I had seen. None of it involved permanent structures, except for the stone altar. Just tents and canvas pavilions. Discerning which of those shelters might harbor a prisoner was my first challenge.

A dull ache grew in the thigh where I had taken the arrow on our recent retreat. Truth be told, deep breathing was not my favorite experience yet either. But I ignored these, for Curunith's sake.

Perhaps our best hope was to fly in, grab the tent Curunith occupied, and remove the canvas in a first pass. From there, we might bank and snatch him up next. However, were he tethered as I had been, we might only succeed in tearing him limb from limb.

I rubbed my forehead. It seemed I had little hope of avoiding some ground reconnaissance, which damaged my odds of success. I understood why Veranna and Majestrin had planned my release before our ultimate retrieval. This time, I had no miraculous invisibility on my side.

This is such a bad idea.

But I have to do it anyway.

I obsessed over possible rescue scenarios, details, plan B, then C, D and so forth, for all the hours we flew, hours I could have been enjoying the quiet of the night, filled only with rushing wind and dragon might.

Maker's mercy, what if they kill Curunith because of me?

I shuddered with each tragic outcome that paraded through my mind, scenarios that crippled thoughts of strategy. More than once, I almost asked Majestrin to turn back. But sometimes the line between cowardice and reason was treacherously blurry.

The wending course of the river Arin glimmered down to my left, shimmering like fish scales in the starlight.

"We draw close, do we not?" I said.

Majestrin nodded. "Yes. But..." He flapped on.

"But what?" My shoulders tightened.

"The air is oddly clean of the dragon-kin's beastly fetor."

"Am I mistaken about the course?"

Majestrin gave me a longsuffering look. "I've flown it enough in the past fortnight to get it right with minimal effort."

My stomach twisted into knots. What had changed? What surprises awaited us?

Majestrin climbed higher in the sky and gained us a broader view of the countryside. A chill crept into my bones. He stopped flapping and instead adopted a circular glide.

I scanned the meadow below. "Did you spot something?"

"No, Captain," Majestrin said. "It's what I no longer see."

I squinted at the ground further. The meadow was churned and beaten at intervals. Dark smudges marked the places fires once burned. A bare platform of stone, bloodstained at its center, stood alone in the emptiness.

The dragon-kin encampment was gone.

12

HOSTAGE

I LEAPT from Majestrin's back before he had even touched his forelimbs to the ground. I dug my fingers into my scalp as I spun and surveyed the landscape around me. There was no mistaking the clear evidence of the encampment. Wagon tracks, forgotten tent pegs, bones and leavings littered my surroundings. I circled the perimeter. Twice, just to be sure.

Majestrin eased up beside me as I stared into the shadow of the woods.

"They've moved to another location," he whispered, not so much as a statement of fact as of sympathy.

"But not as a unit," I said. "There is no evidence of a group departure. Even a troupe as small as five hundred would cut a swath in moving, but as best I can see, these villains have chosen to disperse."

I kicked a charred chunk of wood into the undergrowth. What a grand goose chase this had turned out to be. For all I knew, Veranna and Majestrin's rescue had prompted them to scatter. I had managed to leave Curunith behind a second time.

"With all the canopy, the possibility of us learning much more from the air is minimal," Majestrin said. "I'm sorry."

I propped my forehead in my hand. "No need for you to apologize, Majestrin. It is in no way your fault I asked you to fly me to a dead end."

The dragon looked me in the eye, drew a quick breath, but then shook his head slightly. "We'd best get you home, then. No use being truant because of a situation you have no power over."

After a long stare across the barren clearing, I sighed. "All right. We can go. I might even catch a few hours of sleep before I get to babysit Mithveranon in the morning."

We lifted off once again, and for at least the first hour of our flight back toward Delsinon, I strained my sight after any hints the blasted dragon-kin moved in the lands below. The only signs of life I caught in my scrutiny were my own people's roadway guard stations. At least the abominable lizards had not harried these unassuming servants.

When we arrived at the city, Majestrin alighted on the battlement we had established as our meeting and departure place. I slid from his back and offered him a nod of farewell. The soft expression in his green eyes comforted me that he required nothing more. He departed in a leathery rush of wing beats.

I strode slowly along the battlement, taking in the quiet sights of the fortress in repose. Few windows glowed with light, and even those that did were dim. I allowed the soft breeze of the summer's wee hours to soothe away the sting of failure that dogged me from my fruitless journey.

"Who goes there?" a voice blurted.

I snapped my head left, my heart hammering at the jarring assault upon the silence. My pulse slowed within seconds, however. Just a soldier on patrol, one who would have no opinion about my presence here. I met his gaze with a nonchalant smirk.

"Forgive me, Captain." The soldier bowed in salute to my rank.

"No need," I replied. "Carry on."

I passed him and continued my stroll along the parapet,

turning corner after corner, rounding turrets and drinking in the starlight. As I stepped under the shadow of a balcony overhead, however, my breath caught in my throat. A figure in the castle guard's livery lay slumped upon the battlement a dozen paces ahead. A strange odor lingered in the air, something both sulfurous and cloying at the same time, faint but uncanny.

I jogged to the soldier and turned him over. He was unscathed, though completely unresponsive to my touch. As I examined his face, I recognized him as one of the soldiers left in charge of Mithveranon during the hours of repose.

The hair on my arms prickled. Some devilry was at work here. Amidst the unfamiliar scents, an acrid odor also made the inside of my nose burn, ever so slightly. I leapt to my feet and scanned the area.

A flurry of distant activity, more the rumor of it than anything I could truly see from my position, tugged at my peripheral vision. I squinted over the battlement, across the inner bailey and toward the outer wall. Had I glimpsed something? Or perhaps just the play of deeper darkness upon the ground as a wisp of cloud passed over the face of the moon.

At that moment, by warrior's instinct alone, I flinched. The *whoosh* of a speeding shaft flew past my ear, followed by the chink of metal upon stone. I wheeled. Stuck fast into the castle wall chattered a thick hafted arrow with a parchment fixed around it. I reached for the scroll, but the red wax seal upon it gave me pause. I drew my hand back. The risk of opening any document bearing the gargoyle's head insignia of Queldurik was too great for even my taste.

Not a quarter hour later, the Royal Wing of the fortress had exploded into a hive of activity. The corridor outside the Royal Chambers bustled with Blackwatch, castle guard, and royalty alike. A sole monument of stillness amidst the chaos, however, knelt the queen of our people. Her porcelain face oddly stoic, she cradled the child Prince Saran-lithian, who wailed, inconsolable.

"Make way, Captain," one of the intelligence soldiers said. He and a companion crept along, scrutinizing the floor for heaven knew what.

I shuffled to the wall and leaned against it.

"There's really no reason for you to remain," he continued. "Would you not rather return to your quarters at this exhausting hour?"

"No reason?" I huffed. "The point that I am the only elf who saw anything amiss does not dictate my presence?"

"We can send for you if—"

A pair of bronze doors to my left swung open—the doors to the royal treasury. Galdurith stepped out, the parchment I had seen fired into the wall clenched in his white-knuckled hand.

"Well, Major, what does it say?" I asked.

"Heaven and earth, Captain, can you not keep your nose out of it?" The major raised a despairing palm to the sky. "The Blackwatch have this matter well in hand."

The queen rose slowly, pressing her son's face to her side as he moaned. His hysteria garbled his woe, though I swore some of his sobbed words included "father."

"The Blackwatch has this well in hand, Major?" Her Majesty said in a tone so even and cold it sent a shiver from my scalp to the tips of my toes. "Just as it was no cause for concern that a half-dozen talismans of passage have gone missing since the tournament?" She stepped closer to me, placing a trembling hand on my cheek. "Would that we could have had you for king's champion, young Vinyanel."

I hoped my fury obscured my bewilderment. I glanced back and forth between the major and the queen, stalling for the right words to fit a tight position. To my relief, the queen spoke first.

"My husband..." She paused and smoothed her hair, then surveyed the inhabitants of the corridor. "His Majesty High King Saransaeloth—has been taken hostage by the dragon-kin."

My stomach plummeted into my boots. Another hostage? And with their troops dispersed, where would we even begin to look?

"And so a clue about their presence within our borders emerges," Major Emynon said.

The heat of fury surged into my cheeks. But against its goading, I held my tongue, lest I jeopardize any impact I might have on the mess in our laps.

The queen turned to Galdurith. "And what of the treasury break-in?"

Galdurith cleared his throat. He cast his gaze to the floor for a long moment before meeting the queen's eyes again. "Only one item has been determined gone, Your Majesty."

She waited, her lips pinched into a line.

"The Chalice of Gherag-Tal," the major added.

"What?" I roared. "How is that possible? To hold the thing for only a month before it slips from our grasp again?"

To the major's profound shock, I snatched the parchment from his hand before he tightened his fingers enough to prevent me. I snapped the scroll open and scanned the message contained within as quickly as I could digest the contents. "So, they retreat, the cowards, holding His Majesty's life as a shield on their backs."

"But the contract you hold explains they will release His Majesty as soon as they have retreated to their fortress, chalice in hand, provided we make no chase," Galdurith added.

I threw the parchment to the floor. "And you would take these dung heaps with scales at their word? Their very existence arose from the oath-breaking and kin-slaying of old! And their fortress? They should not even *be* on the mainland of Argent, so clearly larger machinations are in motion. Tell me you are not so naïve, Major."

We locked gazes as the hall fell silent. Every eye was trained upon us.

"Not at all, Captain, but we must tread with more caution than perhaps would be the inclination of a hot-headed young celebrity." Emynon took a firm step toward me, his fists clenched in bristling defiance.

"I have no problem with caution, *Major*, but I must ask, who among the soldiers of our people has faced these enemies, and has lived to tell the tale?" I folded my arms across my chest and settled my weight back on one leg.

"Lived, yes, but at what cost?" The major spoke in a low voice, each word brimming with accusation.

I pulled back a fist. The population of the hall gasped as one, but mingled with their outcry came a familiar sound. Tiny bells.

I dropped my head back and clasped my fingers behind my neck.

"Saved by the prophetess again," Emynon muttered as he marched past me, his shoulder grazing mine. "Veranna, it may not be safe here. I do not yet have word if the perimeter is secure. You should have sent a page."

"It's all right, Galdurith. I prefer to report myself."

"So, you come to join the fray, Prophetess?" I said, my blood still at a good simmer.

"We shall have more than enough conflict before us without sowing it amidst ourselves." She placed herself between the major and me. "I come to inform you that Mithveranon is not in his quarters."

"Thank you for the information, Veranna," the major said.

"But please, don't put yourself at any further risk." He sent a pair of soldiers to further scour the champion's room.

"Mithveranon..." *My Maker, Mithveranon!* A sick roiling welled in my gut. "Where was he during the time His Majesty suffered abduction?"

"Taking his repose. We suspected the intruders had rendered him unconscious like they did the wall guard, to prevent him from protecting the king." Galdurith raked his fingers through thick, sandy locks already tousled with stress. "Not that I owe you any explanation. I don't even know why I'm answering you."

The truth of matters slammed into me like a jousting charger. Shards and notches, I had played right into it.

"Veranna." I grabbed her shoulders. "You kept warning me that Mithveranon gave you an uneasy feeling. Can you explain that any better?"

Her eyes rounded. "I...I sensed he had Thaumaturgy gifts, but...but he always seemed so guarded. And sharp-edged. It's hard to put into words."

I threw my hands into the air. Could I have been any more stupid? The bastard had baited me away from the keep, and surprise! While I was gone, the king, his champion, and the Chalice went missing.

"Sir," one of the Blackwatch soldiers said to Emynon. "I can organize a search for Mithveranon's body."

"His *body*?" My glance pinged from soldier to soldier. "You clearly have not pieced together what is going on here. Dragon-kin within our borders. Talismans missing. Two versions, one dead and one living, of the same elf. And His Majesty's champion, not bleeding on the royal chamber floor, but simply unfound?"

The errand runner that dashed into the wing interrupted my thought.

With a bow to the major, the runner said, "Sir, we can get no report of traffic at the west gate, for the sentries there lay unconscious, much like the patrolman Captain Ecleriast discovered."

"And so the sovereign of the Delsin departs, unseen and perhaps beyond hope of pursuit." The queen hugged the prince closer to her side. "Our vigilance has grown drowsy of late."

The major spun and smacked the wall in his frustration, but Veranna laid a slender hand upon his shoulder.

"There is no way you might have foreseen this, Galdurith," she said.

I spoke through my teeth. "Apparently Her Majesty does not entirely agree."

Emynon did not look at me, but said in a low growl, "I shall say this one more time, *Captain* Ecleriast: this is none of your concern. Go to your horses, your quarters, wherever. I am certain your unit will be summoned for orders if there is anything for which they are needed."

"None of my concern?" I thundered. "In the winning of that Chalice, I lost more excellent soldiers than I care to count, two of them dearer to me than kin. If for nothing else but to honor their memory, this bungling of security concerns me to the utmost."

Galdurith wheeled upon me, his face livid. "Perhaps, Captain," the major bellowed, "if you would at least try to be even moderately likable, you would have some friends left here in Delsinon to console you over the companions you lost in the field!"

His words stung like a slap to the face, but I dared not admit their potency. With a last, scathing glare, I spun and marched from the wing, slamming the door behind me.

I stomped across the fortress grounds toward my quarters, livid Emynon's insult had unnerved me enough to prevent my further accusations of Curunith's abandonment in the field. Or had Curunith's whereabouts also been a ruse? I threw the door to my quarters open and tromped inside. After wrenching my pack from my shoulders, I flung it on my bunk with a clatter, then I yanked my scabbard from the frog. I clutched it in my hands, but I found that they shook. My heart thundered, and beads of sweat rose on my brow.

What could Creo's design be in all this? To undo the work my squadron and I had fought so hard to complete? If he wanted me to serve him, he would do well to make my efforts seem less futile. And why...why could I not remember how, precisely I lost my comrades? The black shroud over our retreat hung over me like a specter, waiting to fell me the moment I let my guard down.

I re-belted the sword and swept a cloak over my shoulders. No, I would not stand aside while the Blackwatch continued to blunder along. Just as I prepared to burst from the room, I heard a soft rapping upon my door.

I swung it open, only to set my jaw at the sight of the major standing in my doorway. He held his chin high, but did not meet my gaze.

"Captain, Her Majesty wishes you to accompany my unit in the pursuit of King Saransaeloth," he began quietly. "Your experience with the enemy renders you"—he paused as if the words stuck in his throat—"invaluable to the effort."

The prospect of once again facing dragon-kin sped my heart further, and motes began to flash at the edges of my vision. But for this vile betrayal, for being played as a fool, I would see this through. I swallowed.

"When do we march?"

"As soon as you are ready." The major turned to depart, but hesitated. "And Captain? Please accept my apologies for my lack of professionalism before. It will not happen again." His words had a wooden quality.

I offered a stiff nod. "See you in the outer bailey."

A s I stepped into the moonlit outer bailey, already a dozen Blackwatch soldiers, dour-faced and shrouded in sable uniforms, assembled in the place. The major and Veranna stood in close proximity, speaking in tones too quiet for me to hear. Not that I necessarily wanted to know what either said, with the way Veranna's hand rested upon the major's lapel and the unwavering connection in their gazes. They spoke quick words until the major jerked his head my direction. Veranna clamped her lips shut.

"A fond farewell?" I said, an unrestrained acerbic edge on my tone.

Veranna smiled. "Not quite yet, Vinyanel. We were just talking about you."

At least she was honest.

"I'm sure you shall be pleased to learn that I shall only accompany you up until the final phase of this mission," Veranna continued.

"That is only logical," I replied. "A maneuver of this level of sensitivity is no place for a civilian female with no weapons training."

"I am gratified that we agree, Captain. However, a Thaumaturgist will be needed."

The way she eyed me as she said this tempted me to squirm. I said nothing for fear of betraying my discomfort. My glance darted around the small assembly in search of some elf I knew to be one of Creo's magically-gifted servants. But no, only the major's intelligence unit stood at the ready.

"So, I hope you have a clear head for learning as we travel to catch up to the dragon-kin," Veranna added. "If there are to be any Virtusen channeled on this mission, young Windrider, they shall come through you."

13

MITHVERANON'S TRAIL

"Prophetess, are you daft?" I snorted.

I had officially entered territory where a profound lack of expertise threatened to leave me looking inept. The logical response was to belittle the person who had placed me in this awkward spot.

Veranna stared at me, with a tilt of her head and crinkle in her brow. I heard the Major's slow intake of breath, but I did not wait for him to embark upon his chivalric duty to intervene upon the prophetess's behalf.

"I know you will correct me if I am wrong," I continued, "but I was under the distinct impression that Thaumaturgy was an inherent gifting. How, exactly, is this captain of cavalry supposed to assume the duty that typically falls to priests or prophets of Creo?"

A bemused expression replaced Veranna's confusion. "Clearly, Creo has chosen not to enlighten you as to what happened while I lay bound to the sacrifice altar." Her unwavering gaze tightened upon me, forcing a rush of blood to my cheeks.

"And I suppose you shall revel in lording this knowledge over me." I pursed my lips. "Do all you mentor types relish this sort of power struggle? To withhold elusive and imperative information just to see your pupils squirm?"

Veranna took a single step back. "When have I ever done so?"

"When have you not?"

Emynon spoke through a clenched jaw. "That's enough, Ecleriast."

"Captain, do you question my teaching technique?" Veranna stared, her expression stuck somewhere between astonishment and fury.

"I do, Prophetess." I lowered my chin, and now it was I who bored into her with a drilling stare. "*Teach with a heart of humility, for it opens the ears of those who listen.*"

Veranna's jaw dropped. "And now you presume to fling Creo's holy word at me as a weapon?"

I was unprepared for the tears that sprang to Veranna's eyes, but I held my ground. The bright call of a silver trumpet arrested my next barbed comment.

"Sounds to me like the end of the round, Captain," Galdurith said. He took Veranna's arm and steered her gently away from me. Over his shoulder he added, "We move out. And if you know what's good for you, keep your distance."

T he dark horse charged over dale and through glen, tearing clods of turf up with every frenzied, desperate hoof beat. Still, the elven king's champion flogged the beast with the loose ends of the reins, swinging them with a whistle to crack against each side of the horse's foaming neck. The moon set. The sun crested the horizon and rode into the sky, and yet they pressed onward.

More and more, the mount's tight, shortened strides faltered. Cursed nag. Only after the horse tumbled headlong into a gully, throwing him to the ground, did he relent. He wrenched his pack from the cantle of the saddle and marched off, leaving the heaving beast to groan in its agony. It had served its purpose.

By the late afternoon of the next day, he reached the newly pitched dragon-kin camp. Quiet hung over the tents and pavilions. The braziers upon his Holy Eminence's altar had been left to burn to a smolder. Some had even gone cold. The champion scowled.

He marched straight for Scitherias's scarlet tent. The flap snapped as he threw it aside and stepped through.

Scitherias raised his eyes from the map spread under his talons, a map that looked to encompass all the western half of Argent. "We have standards of etiquette here, fool. I hope you have come to report your success to me."

He folded his arms. "You have obligations to Queldurik for the victories he has granted you. When you neglect those simple commands, I'm less than wont to observe your childish rules of posturing."

Scitherias scoffed. "I know who my liege lord is, even if the demon worshipers have forgotten the ultimate source of the powers we wield. I'm unimpressed by Queldurik, the middleman."

The one disguised as Mithveranon winced as though stricken. "I'll not stand for blasphemy. You risk tempting His Eminence to withhold the very prize you sent me after."

"Your threats are empty. If nothing else, I know Queldurik is good for his word." Scitherias dipped his quill in a bottle of ink and scratched a few notes on his map. "And by the way, the rubbish heap? Really? Any success you've had strikes me as more luck than skill, with that sloppy choice so early on."

"Disposing of a body in the midst of a festival has its obstacles," he said. "The blasted Delsin are always awake."

"You tire me with your excuses. Do you have the Chalice?" Scitherias said.

Smoldering hatred flared in his gut as he pulled the Chalice of Gherag-tal from his pack and held it forth. "I have brought what you asked, and I assume the abductors have already arrived with the greater spoils."

"And the talisman. You'll have no further need of it."

He pulled the silver chain bearing the scroll-and-sword emblem over his head, then handed it to Scitherias. "Now, release me from this repugnant disguise."

A low chuckle that slowly piled upon itself until it grew into uproarious laughter overcame Scitherias. "Just who is the binder, and who is the slave? Or have you forgotten in your time away from me? No, I am not yet finished with you in your current trappings." His smile evaporated. "Now leave my tent before my sense of humor runs out."

Major Emynon's detachment rode at a laborious pace, following his trackers as they sorted periodic three-toed tracks from older foot traffic beyond Delsinon's gates. A pack of hunting hounds snuffled in the lead to provide a heading when footprints failed. Majestrin and I drifted along, occasionally gaining some height, more for the sake of killing time while the Blackwatch tracked than gaining any additional information. I squirmed in Majestrin's newly-crafted saddle. At this rate, His Majesty would have grown old and languished in their keeping before we made any appreciable gains on the abductors.

And yet another burr dug at me—what of Curunith? I could not safely raise the question of his presence without causing an uproar. But would also not return home from this mission without seeing to his liberation. No matter which way I turned the matter in my mind, a clear course of action remained beyond sight.

Veranna kept her distance from me as we rode, and any time I looked her way, she turned her own gaze as far from mine as possible. Thaumaurgist. Me? The mere thought made my breath short. At intervals, I drew my copy of *The Tree* from my pack, but I thumbed through the pages at a loss. What a waste of precious time. Was there anything I was actually equipped to do well for this excursion? The thorny barbs of inefficiency drove back my distaste for conversation with her.

I steered Majestrin to Veranna's side of the phalanx of soldiers. "I believe you had some statutes to impress upon me with regard to Creo's power?"

She regarded me through narrowed eyes. "You might find the lesson too abrasive, Captain."

With a huff, I shook my head. "Let us not play games, Prophetess. I have not the slightest notion how to either recognize Creo's will in a matter such as this or how to enact his Virtusen when he calls for them. Can we not bury our grievances for the sake of the stakes?"

"I could fill a cemetery with the grievances I've buried for your sake over the weeks since we met," Veranna said.

"Then you have clearly taken the emotional steps necessary to move on from here." I extended my book to her. "Show me how to begin."

Veranna gaped at me. "You can figure it out for yourself, Captain. I did, when no one would teach me." She reined her horse aside.

Impossible female.

I called after her, "I suppose I shall retract my suggestion Emynon decorate you for longsuffering." An ache spread through my jaw from my grinding molars.

"Take heart, Captain," Majestrin said in a low voice. "*The righteous desires of the fervent, these I shall enact with my miracles. Even unwitting, my servant shall summon forth my glory.*"

"That is all well and good, Majestrin," I said, my jaw unmoving. "But in the coming situation, I would very much rather be *witting*, if I have a say."

"Perhaps you shall keep this discomfiture in mind, the next time it occurs to you to fling insults."

As the first day of our march saw the purple glow of evening, I paced the northern edge of camp. A Blackwatch scout materialized out of the foliage and jogged through our small ring of tents. He stopped when he found Emynon.

"Major, I come to report." He bowed, fist over his heart.

Emynon returned his salute and nodded.

"Sir, we have some concrete information at last, just shy of a league distant," the scout said. "There is a dead horse, out of the king's stables, judging by his tack. And from there, it appears a rider continued on foot."

"A possible abductor," the major said.

My pulse quickened. Two possibilities loomed in my mind.

I approached Emynon as well. "How long dead is the horse?"

The scout furrowed his brow at me. "Uh...not very? I did not evaluate it extensively."

I pursed my lips. A quick consideration of geography, our current location, and the point where I departed Curunith's company lessened the chances the animal the scout found might be my comrade's. "I'm willing to wager that trail leads to our so-called king's champion."

"So-called?" The major arched an eyebrow. "You discount the equally plausible scenario that Mithveranon rode out to fulfill his duty to protect His Majesty. What reason do you have to cast him in the worst possible light?"

I clapped a palm to my forehead. "Suspicion is the only reasonable response to the discovery of a corpse at the tournament. Does anyone truly contest the likelihood of foul play involving Mithveranon?"

"I refuse to take the path of accusation until we have actual evidence." Galdurith shifted his focus to the scout. "How old do you deem this trail?"

"Not more than a half-day, sir."

"What of the dragon-kin tracks?" I straightened my sword belt.

"I fear we lost those at the creek crossing a few leagues back, sir," the scout said.

"Show me the horse," I said.

The scout turned a questioning look to Emynon.

He waved the scout on. "Humor the captain."

I shot Emynon a disgusted look as I tailed the scout back into the cover of the trees. We followed a game trail churned by shod hooves, and all the while, my nerves tingled on edge. Only the evening chatter of birds reached our ears along our route, even though I thought I heard, more than once, phantom footfalls nearby. Through the trees, I spied a dark, mounded shape on the ground. Not bay of coat, as Curunith's mount had been, but black —a courser.

The sight of the horse's body sent a surge of fire through my flesh. The dried, matted hair on the beast's neck and flanks rumored hard use, as did raw patches on his shoulders and rump. His bit had torn his mouth to mangled shreds. Flies crawled over the ragged lips. The mount had served well when rightly used in the tournament arena and borne his rider to victory. His reward: to be ridden to death and left as carrion in the far reaches of the woodlands.

"Very well. I have discovered all I needed." I turned and led the way back to camp. "Send a pair of privates to bury this animal."

I marched straight to Emynon. "Your mounts can brook further pursuit, they've had an easy day. I say we follow this new trail as soon as Mithveranon's horse is properly managed."

"You're positive the beast was his?" Emynon said.

"Major, if there is anything I know, it is horses. Why must you question me at every turn?"

The major sighed, and his glance lingered on Veranna's sleeping form where she had collapsed soon after we made camp.

"You should send her back to Delsinon," I said. "What use is having her here to risk injury or death?"

"You assume I have any say in whether she comes or goes." Emynon rubbed his forehead. "This could very well end up being a diversion. I understand you're familiar with the notion."

And so Emynon's promise of professionalism evaporated, leaving in its place a roiling uncertainty about how much he knew of my reasoning for leaving Delsinon the night of the king's abduction.

"This is no rabbit trail," I said. "Between Veranna's unease about Mithveranon and my own misgivings, I am certain that following this trail will lead us to answers."

Emynon met my gaze for a long moment. "Very well. Best not to grant them any more lead." He turned to the scout. "Sound the move."

s the night passed and so the first half of the next day, we kept a sharp eye on the trail, loath to lose it in case the tracks should waver into deeper cover. I rolled my shoulders and neck, stiff from the long stretches in the saddle. Our brief pauses on the trail had offered us little in the way of repose, but Emynon's soldiers exhibited thorough training. By rotating which soldiers caught rest while others watched, they all remained attentive and methodical despite the length of the hunt. I, on the rare occasions I managed to still my mind enough to do so, rested in the saddle, which proved one of the advantages of having a mount that did not need my guidance.

The midday had waned into afternoon when our advance scouts came riding toward us at speed. Their tabards were splattered with blood, and one of the scouts' cheeks bore three red claw gouges. They each hauled a limp soldier behind them.

"Soldiers, report," I said when they drew near enough.

"Perimeter guards. Dragon-kin," the lead scout said. "Two leagues ahead. Privates Feynir and Illdrin need the medics."

From the rear of our column, two elves ran up with a stretcher, while the advance scouts lowered their comrades to the ground. I swept my glance over the wounded. Their injuries— primarily bruising to their faces and heads, suggested to me perhaps the dragon-kin intended to take prisoners more than exterminate. The medics leaned in and blocked my further investigation.

"And how did your encounter play out?" Emynon asked.

The lead scout swept a hand across his perspiring brow. "We eliminated the guards. Brutal, these monsters are, if a little sluggish on the draw."

"It was likely the end of a daytime watch," I said. "The only time they are sluggish is when they are sun-sick."

Emynon furrowed his brow at his scouts. "And yet, presumably sun-sick, they downed two of you?"

"Had the guards been any less impaired, I wager you would be four men down and we would be facing a charge of demon worshippers upon our remaining column." I paced. "What further can you tell us?"

The injured scout stretched taller in his saddle. "We have sighted His Majesty within the camp. He appears to be unharmed, but bound and under heavy guard."

"We should call a halt." I told Emynon. "Send the horses with the wranglers, set the canopy encampment and the camouflage." I clenched my fists and turned on my heel to pace back. "If our luck holds, we might further stake out the scenario before we make our move. Not before dawn, if we can avoid notice until then."

Emynon nodded. "I doubt we have that much time before they investigate the loss of their guards."

My back prickled with sweat. "Indeed, which is why it is imperative we avoid their notice tonight. We must control the timing of our maneuvers—when we begin to harry and distract. Just enough potshotting to get the king clear so Majestrin can take him home."

"And you are sure His Majesty will be entirely...safe...with Majestrin?" Emynon cast a nervous glance over Majestrin's length.

"Whatever elf travels with Majestrin will be far safer than any of us," I replied.

Veranna leaned back on her hands and savored the chill of stone cooling her palms. She tilted her chin higher to gaze into the deepening purple of the evening sky, where celestial bodies winked into view, one glimmering pinprick at a time.

Downhill from her rocky stargazing perch, the soldiers hitched woven hammocks into the canopy of the trees in silence. Some stretched leafy nets under the hammocks, blending the soldiers' hiding places seamlessly into the dense network of branches. They built no fire, but in turns nibbled cold rations instead. Ever since the sighting of the dragon-kin perimeter guards, Galdurith's unit had snapped into a mode of quiet precision, performing their tasks in a practiced flow, underscored by watchfulness and anticipation. Rarely did she indulge in jealousy over the traits that full elves enjoyed that she did not, but at the moment, she longed for the endurance these soldiers had. She stifled a yawn. Each of her blinks came slower than the last—oh, to allow her eyes to remain shut.

Outside their militaristic choreography, Vinyanel leaned against a tree. His fingers absently traced the worn leather that wrapped the grip of his sword. The muscles around his eyes tightened, his teeth ground. Veranna forced her gaze back to the heavens.

A faint buzzing sensation awoke across Veranna's scalp and spread down her neck to her arms. It intensified, moment by moment. She cast her glance all about the wilderness below her rocky perch. Her hands clenched of their own accord.

The buzzing grew to an electrified tremor over her entire body, so powerful she always feared she shook, though these sensations had yet to be visible to anyone else. Occasional zaps and sparks punctuated the feeling.

Ah, Majestrin returns.

Veranna searched the sky, and indeed the silver dragon approached from the south. Once he had flown within a stone's throw, the sparking in Veranna's flesh washed away. Majestrin met her glance and alighted not beside Vinyanel, but on the stony slope below her seat.

"Prophetess," Majestrin said, "It's time for you to depart for the position Galdurith has set for you."

She cocked her head. "But Vinyanel said they wouldn't engage the dragon-kin until tomorrow."

"That doesn't mean the dragon-kin won't discover them first," Majestrin said. "You'll have guards—there's no reason to be afraid."

"I'm not afraid." Veranna unclenched her fists.

Majestrin's lip curled. He blinked slowly. "Come. Don't complicate Galdurith and Vinyanel's task."

Veranna sighed and rose. She picked her way down to the dragon. "Is it walking distance?"

The dragon's shoulders slumped. "I suppose."

After walking beside Majestrin until the Blackwatch camp had vanished, Veranna released a sigh. "You're confident this strategy will succeed and get everyone back to Delsinon alive, right?"

Majestrin's gaze wandered into the distance. "Everyone? I do hope we have such fortune, but the chances of losing some of this squadron are real indeed."

"But you'll keep Vinyanel from hanging himself, right?"

The dragon curved his neck around to quirk a brow at Veranna. "One might say he has already been subjected to such risk, having been deemed Thaumaturgist with no instruction in specific Virtusen."

Veranna brought her feet together. "That's not fair. I'm just the messenger. He was the one to react by calling me daft, haughty, and a poor teacher in the same breath."

"And so the best response, as the more spiritually mature member of the partnership, was to retract all instruction on the way to a mission where he would need every tool possible for success?"

Veranna drew a breath and pinched her lips together. She and Majestrin pressed on through the rough undergrowth. Brambles caught in her long hair and snagged her clothes continually. *Creo, how am I supposed to get Vinyanel to see me as worthy of respect? I can't teach him without that.* Tears stung her tired eyes. A branch of thorns whipped across her face, and when she raised her hand to the lash, her fingers came back smeared with blood. She grimaced.

Majestrin spoke in a low voice. "Had we flown, your face wouldn't be bleeding and you'd already be in bed."

Veranna released a little, sardonic laugh. *Though the path is fraught with fear, it may yet be the best route.*

"Majestrin, when you return to Vinyanel, assure him that the power he needs is his to implore of the Maker."

The dragon sidled onward, silent for many strides, but a spark of contemplation working in his eyes. "What gives you that impression?"

"The point I was going to make to Vinyanel, before he erupted at me, was that in the moment the dragon-kin sought to burn me on the altar to Queldurik, it was a Virtus that came through him that kept the fuel from lighting." Veranna plucked a strand of hair from sticking to her smeared cheek. "He has already performed a work of Thaumaturgy, even if he did not recognize it."

"Interesting," Majestrin said. "I was unaware that was possible."

Veranna rolled her eyes, and a nervous laugh escaped her. "For most mere mortals, it's not." With a hesitant gesture, she reached out, paused, then laid her hand on Majestrin's silver scales.

The dragon slowed to a stop and met her gaze. Prickles of sweat dewed on the small of Veranna's back, and heat ran into her cheeks.

"The amount of power he could wield is terrifying," she whispered. "The two of you together? Staggering. And Creo asks me to cultivate this blindly. I have no foresight as to the Maker's purpose."

Soft sympathy welled in Majestrin's eyes, and he lowered his eyelids a fraction. "You fear what you will unleash on an unprepared world should you misstep in this summons."

Veranna only bit her lip and nodded.

"Well," the dragon said, "I cannot speak to the Maker's purposes, but to start, it may help you to learn and to model one thing."

She implored with expression alone, mistrustful of her voice.

"You don't have to be incorrigible to be strong."

14

INTERCEPTION

THE SUN CRESTED the distant horizon of rolling hills as I sat upon Majestrin's back. It rose red as wrath this morning, casting what remained of the dragon-kin camp in an ominous fiery glow. The dragon-kin had packed and loaded their equipment and personnel, and they began to move out in the wee hours, forcing our hand in beginning our reconnaissance earlier than I would have preferred. As far as I knew, detachments of Blackwatch soldiers already harried the marching enemy column and sought to free the king.

That was, if all proceeded as planned. I cracked my knuckles.

"Are you ready, Vinyanel?" Majestrin asked.

I jolted from introspection. "My flesh fills with tremors to begin. Where is that signal?"

"It will come."

"Do you think the Blackwatch have orders to also seek Curunith?"

Majestrin met my eye. "How do the odds of success change if this becomes a double extraction?"

I swallowed my next thought about the Chalice. My frail

hopes were cracking my usual resistance to airing dumb questions.

"Quiet your mind, my friend." Majestrin turned to face the valley before us.

I suppressed a sigh, but also did as Majestrin suggested. Soon enough, I would see the glint of light that would summon the dragon and me to swoop in and bear His Majesty home. The wait crawled all over me like a swarm of fire ants. I attempted to quell the sensation by rehearsing what statutes of *The Tree* I thought might place me in the right frame of mind to recognize if Creo bade me channel his power. I admit, I also prayed Veranna was wrong in there being any need for me to do so.

"Majestrin?" The quaver in my voice filled my stomach with nausea. I coughed several times to clear my throat, then brushed at the shoulder of my cloak. "Do you know anything about Thaumaturgy?"

"Not much, Vinyanel."

"Do you suppose there is any chance Veranna is mistaken about her assertion that I have this gift? After all, would this not have been something I might have noticed by now?"

"I have heard stories of those who did not discover such a gifting until their old age." Majestrin shifted beneath me. "So, no, Captain, I don't think Veranna is misguided in this."

"You know more than you are saying aloud." I laced my fingers behind my neck and hung the weight of my arms on them.

"This is the wrong time to plumb those depths."

"You and Veranna keep talking about me, do you not?"

"Perhaps." Majestrin grinned in his unnerving, toothy way. "Funny a dragon should be easier to talk to than an elf. I shall not break her confidence."

I slumped in my seat, then set my mind to inventorying my equipment. Sword? Of course. Shield? On my back. Crossbow? Left shoulder. Quarrels? In the side pouch of the quiver. Daggers?

Well, dagger. On my belt. The snap of a twig off to my right intercepted my attention. Who should emerge from the dense foliage but...

Sir Direllian Mithveranon.

Still in his champion's livery, looking very smudged and tattered.

"Praise my Lord I have found you, Captain!" Mithveranon said, breathless.

"Convenient." I folded my arms.

A stricken look overtook his pale face. "I am sorry I did not have time to report upon my actions, sir, but the king's life was at stake! As his champion and protector, I had to pursue him and his captors at once. But there is no time to explain further. The Blackwatch have blundered, but the dragon-kin forces seem unaware of your presence so far. If we can just—"

I blew out a great gust of breath. "Enough of your blathering!"

"Blathering?" Mithveranon frowned. "I'm trying to offer you a route to extracting His Majesty alive!"

"If you are truly his champion, you should not be here without him!" I thundered.

Mithveranon's features hardened. "Not all of us are so fortunate to have your level of talent and training, Captain. I cannot save him alone."

"But you assert we can succeed together?"

Mithveranon nodded.

Majestrin swung his head over to stare Mithveranon in the face. "Then lead on."

Mithveranon dropped back a step. "Oh heavens, the moment they see you they'll slit the king's throat." He met my gaze. "The dragon will have to stay." His voice trembled even as he insisted. "We have no hope of making a stealthy approach with him. And stealth is all that is left to us." He broke into a jog, back the way he had come. "I cannot delay further. Follow or not."

I slid from Majestrin's back. "Can you pick up the king without my help?" I whispered.

"Vinyanel, what are you planning?" Majestrin turned a skeptical eye toward Mithveranon.

"I have had more than enough mysteries surrounding this king's champion. I will follow." I clapped the dragon on his scaly side, then turned to follow the path of Mithveranon's swift retreat. "When you see the signal, go, with or without me," I called over my shoulder.

As we ran through the glades that stood between Majestrin's hilltop perch and the encampment remnants below, I scrutinized Mithveranon's gait, wary that he should draw a weapon. Though he did not, I ran with my hand on my hilt. "Explain in what way the rescue has been compromised."

"Did not the directive of the dragon-kin insist the Delsin make no pursuit?" Mithveranon replied.

Funny he should know about that, given that he was not present in the corridor discussion of the scroll's contents.

At my lack of response, he continued, his nasal voice pinched with condescension. "Careless scouts, sloppy maneuvers...all these put His Majesty at grave risk."

"The details you offer are damning, King's Champion. As is the fact that you carry no equipment save your sword. You did not leave anything with the horse you killed, that I know."

Mithveranon blustered. "There was no time to so much as grab a bag!"

I snorted. "Tell me, did you take your repose in that uniform, or did you take the time to layer it on once you heard of His Majesty's peril?"

Mithveranon ran a few more paces, then slowed to a stop. He bent over, bracing his hands upon his knees to heave for breath. "I think we've run far enough now," he said through ragged gasps.

I fought the urge to find my blade a new scabbard in Mithveranon's gut. Instead I searched my mind for the right, probing question that would lay bare his treachery beyond doubt.

Mithveranon sprang so suddenly that even my wary nerves failed to respond in time. He latched an iron grip upon my throat. We crashed to the leafy floor. My sword pinned under me, I groped for my signal horn, anything. But the elf's fingers around my windpipe and his body weight atop mine frustrated my struggle.

"Such an arrogant fool to follow me." A horrifying leer twisted his features beyond recognition. "I knew I could count on your overconfidence to lure you from your assigned duty. Those plans might falter with you dead!"

Bereft of a weapon, I grabbed the back of Mithveranon's skull and drove his forehead into my own. Despite my helm, stars still burst across my vision, so I could only imagine the effect the attack might have had upon my bare-headed opponent. His fingers loosened upon my throat just enough for me to kick him off. I rolled. In a single motion, I regained my feet and swept my sword from the scabbard.

To my dismay, Mithveranon rolled backward and also stood, looking far less impaired than I hoped. He drew a sabre from his belt. I raised my sword for the first parry.

The stroke never came. Mithveranon bolted into the under-brush with inhuman speed. At that pace, he would reach the dragon-kin column quickly—too quickly for me to run back for Majestrin.

I charged after the retreating elf.

This was as good a day as any to die.

15

OUTMATCHED

I BARRELED through the forested wilderness, leapt streams, tore through brambles, and forced my muscles to the brink of overexertion as I pursued the retreating Mithveranon. I had chased down enough opponents in my time that it grew clear to me something lent this one speed beyond any mortal fleetness of foot. Fast or not, our sparring during his training had taught me that as long as I could catch him, I could dispatch him. Now, to slow him down.

As I ran, I grabbed for the light crossbow on my back. Though not the weapon of my preference, it was the best option in the circumstances. I fumbled with a quarrel but spared no glance to the weapon as I struggled to load it, lest my pace slow. With a grunt, I cocked the weapon. Only then did I stop. I pulled the crossbow release, and the quarrel sprang for my target. The dart whistled in, then connected with the back of the elf's knee. He staggered.

The quarrel performed the task I required; Mithveranon's limping gait slowed him enough for me to close the gap between us. I exchanged my crossbow for my longsword and shield. As I descended upon my quarry, he wheeled clumsily to catch the arc of my longsword upon his sabre. A tar-black sludge ran down his calf. He groped with his off hand to pull my quarrel from his flesh, but where I expected to see panic, instead his eyes flared, wild and fey. He flung the missile into the dirt. From the corner of my eye, I glimpsed a curl of smoke slithering into the air from the slimed shaft.

He may have been calling himself Direllian Mithveranon. Had an elven appearance. But something was severely amiss with this king's champion.

He circled his sabre and thrust at me; our weapons ground against one another until my blade met his basket hilt. With more strength than he had shown in any of our sparring, my opponent thrust me back. We circled. We wheeled. Every charge I made at him, he met with gritted teeth and a steady hand. I concentrated upon deflecting the tight, flicking motions of his narrow blade, as he sought an opening to sink its point into my flesh. He found no such opening.

I abandoned typical, refined tactics for hacking at his weapon. Perhaps I could sunder the thin strip of steel, or at least jar it out of his hand.

"What's the matter, Vinny?" Mithveranon sneered. "Afraid if I have a weapon in hand that I might put a dent in your girlish face?"

Vinny? Oh, he might have to pay for that.

All thoughts of mercy or discourse cast aside, I bellowed a wordless battle cry and sprang at Mithveranon. To my chagrin, neither my wrath hew nor my signature redoubling availed me in this battle, and yet, neither did my enemy find his way past any guard I threw in his path. I added no more substantial wound than I had already dealt with my crossbow.

The duel dragged on. Sweat soaked my back and brow. Never in my sixty years as a soldier had it taken so long to prevail. My only comfort—my opponent was flagging. I saw it in his eyes. A vague look of desperation grew in his features, even if the pace of his sword strokes never slackened.

"You are a liar and a villain," I bellowed at him between breaths.

I drove him back a few paces, where a protruding tree root snagged his boot. He threw his arms up to save his balance, which gave me just the opening I sought. My sword whistled in a devastating under-hew, and its edge caught Mithveranon beneath his arm, right at the shoulder joint. I felt the familiar drag as my blade severed muscle, tendon, and bone. My opponent's weapon as well as his weapon arm flew away from his body. Black ichor spattered my breastplate.

Mithveranon sank to his knees. He panted, but did not crash to the ground as a dismembered elf would. I angled my sword across his throat.

"It was a lie, was it not?" I said. "That the dragon-kin have Curunith?"

Footsteps from ahead stalled the death blow I had poised to deliver. A smirk twisted the corner of Mithveranon's mouth.

Not far ahead, a tall, opulently garbed dragon-kin emerged from the cover of the undergrowth. He stalked toward me with a leer on his crocodilian face. His tarnished scales, his smug composure I could never mistake.

Lord Scitherias.

Secrecy was a joke in poor taste now. I snatched my signal horn from over my shoulder and blew a shrill blast upon it.

The note cut short as Scitherias waved his hand and the horn launched from my grip to land somewhere in the underbrush.

"You must be very fond of me, Captain Ecleriast, to pay me visits thrice in a matter of weeks," Scitherias said with an unamused smile. "Or else you are one who craves death and simply cannot manage to apprehend it."

I allowed a long pause to hang between us while I mastered

my labored breathing. "Indeed, I sought you for the first of our encounters, but you have now invited my harassment, tarrying here on the land of my people." I threw my shoulders back. "Render unto me all that belongs to the Delsin, as well as the Chalice of Gherag-tal, which no mortal should possess. Take your ragtag collection of demon worshipers back to the Isle of Desolation, and perhaps the elves shall stay their hands in bringing the full force of our army upon you. Defy these demands, and not even the rumor of your force shall return to your kin."

Scitherias guffawed. "So, you come to deliver terms, do you? Your pathetic people will learn the meaning of humbleness forthwith." He turned to Mithveranon, who knelt between us with a bleary look on his face. "Be as you are, my servant, and make an end of this mosquito of a warrior, Ecleriast."

He pointed to the one-armed elf, and instantly, the pale face, the flaxen hair, and the livery of King Saransaeloth crumbled like dry sand and were borne away on the wind, leaving behind an ebony-skinned apparition so dreadful to behold that my stomach churned at the sight. His face was no more than leathery hide stretched over a bony skull, with eyes of flame flickering in deep sockets. A hundred needle-pointed teeth protruded from his mouth, a tangled thicket of pain. He rose, whole as can be, with *two* long arms and spindly, sinewy legs that trembled only a moment before he sprang at me.

Scitherias stood back like a gambler at a cockfight as I blocked the fiend's first assault with my shield. We circled, gauging one another, feinting but withholding attack until I could stand it no more and lunged. The thrust would have skewered any earthly opponent. My sword skittered across its flesh, leaving only a scratch. The droplets of demon's blood that ran down my blade and onto the crosspiece chattered as water does upon a hot pan.

The fiend jabbed in low, but as I intercepted the strike, it swung its other clawed hand over my shield, raking my face and awakening a fire across my cheek. A roar of pain burst from my lungs. I shook my head in an effort to keep my wits. The fight would end quickly, and not in my favor, if I let the augmented pain distract me.

My enemy's claws proved horrific, rending my breastplate like foil in the next strike. Cuts and slashes from my own sword only scored its flesh. I plunged my blade, tip first, and this punched open a rare wound that spouted ichor and stench like boiling pitch.

It repaid my assault with a snapping jaw. Its teeth sank into my shield, and it ripped a chunk away like a lion tearing its kill.

We exchanged further slashes and rakes, and I drew some satisfaction at the fiend's increasing collection of wounds, though for the creature's every gash, I had three. And unlike the beast's otherworldly hide, mine did not roil and bubble and knit itself back together.

The black mist of tunnel vision encroached upon the edges of my awareness. The metallic smell of my own blood filled my nostrils. Every wound the fiend had dealt me flamed with searing pain. Waves of nausea crashed over me.

With a ferocious swipe, the fiend bashed my forearm, and to my horror, my blade jangled from my sweaty, bloody, weakened grasp, to land several yards to my left. It stabbed into the earth to stand in full view, but mockingly out of reach.

Somewhere in the mist of my ever-darkening vision, Scitherias laughed. "Finish it, slave. Really, Ecleriast...I thought you would offer better sport than this."

If the draconic lord had hoped to demoralize me with his mockery, he failed. A surge of feral mania boiled up from my inmost being. I would destroy Scitherias's slave with my bare hands, if need be.

The fiend lunged, mouth gaping. I grappled its shoulders and held it back, but still, its putrid, hot breath clouded over my jaw and throat. I threw my weight to the side, we crashed to the ground. We rolled. Kicked. Punched. A trail of mingled black ichor and red blood stained the clearing.

Through it all, however, my sword remained ever in my hazy peripheral vision. With every roll, I blundered us closer to the weapon.

The creature scrambled and clutched. It drove bony fingers under my helm and grabbed a tangle of my hair. The sword stood just inches from reach. With all the strength that remained in my shield arm, I drove my shield at the creature. The bash knocked my enemy back, though the ripping pain in my scalp told me a chunk of my hair went with him.

I rolled to my knees, reached out, and caught hold of my hilt once again. I forced my blurring vision to focus on the fiend as it swayed where it sat. Stunned. My bicep screamed in protest as I lifted the weight of the sword once again.

"In Creo's mighty name, I banish you to the abyss, servant of darkness!"

I plunged my weapon between the eyes of the demon, just as he lifted a horrified glance to me. My sword shuddered so violently that it shook from my hand again. In a blaze of red, the creature exploded into a shower of ash and was no more.

I panted, my muscles going slack. I turned a sluggish gaze to Scitherias, who stood with arms folded and a deadly scowl pulling at his mouth.

"A perfect example of what happens when you delegate to the chattel of a fake," he muttered to himself. "Very well, Ecleriast. If you are so determined to die at my hand alone, I shan't deny you such a privilege."

I heaved myself to my feet, using my sword as a crutch. I swung the tatters of my shield in front of me, while Scitherias wove his hands in an intricate pattern before him. Sparking runes of bilious green formed in the air before him. I got the distinct impression, no matter the condition of my shield, it would be little help.

Majestrin squinted after Vinyanel and Mithveranon as the two elves vanished under the cover of foliage.

"Creo, protect him, even in his foolhardiness," the dragon whispered. His long neck drooped as he turned back to watch for the Blackwatch's signal. Surely Vinyanel saw Mithveranon's presence was likely nothing better than a trap. He had the wits to outsmart the slippery fellow, if only he would remember to use them. More likely, he would try brawn first. Majestrin sighed, a silver cloud of cold mist curling from his nostrils.

The morning sun rode higher, and the lands around Majestrin shed their vermilion mantle to exchange them for the clinging mists that lingered in low places during early morning. Had one of those banks of fog obscured the flash for which he waited? No. The major would know better. He hoped.

"I spend too much time with that high-strung elf!" Majestrin chuckled to himself. "When was the last time I worried, before I met him? His fretfulness must be contagious."

A wink of white light flashed in the distant northwest. Two more flashes, in rapid succession. Vinyanel had not returned. The elf had instructed Majestrin should go without him, if need be. To follow that instruction seemed more dubious now that the signal insisted. How long had it been since Majestrin had done more than hunt the northern wilderness and drowse in his den, blissfully unaware of the goings-on of men or elves? But Creo's divine summons had been unmistakable, and when the prophetess had appeared at the mouth of his abode, he could no longer play at mulling it over. The ferocious intensity of Vinyanel's untapped magical signature sealed Majestrin's conviction, however reluctant.

After two more flashes, Majestrin took another deep, preparatory breath, then launched from his hilltop perch.

The dragon stretched long and flat, skimming the treetops as he shot like a ballista bolt for the signal. Only moments after the takeoff, a shrill note, short but not distant, cut through the sounds of morning.

Majestrin faltered. The horn call came from the direction Vinyanel and Mithveranon had gone, and the note had been cut shorter than any player might have intended. His focus flicked between his destination and his distraction. As Vinyanel's mount and partner in battle, could he, in good conscience, ignore a possible threat to his rider?

Majestrin closed his eyes in search of clarity. The mission. That is what Vinyanel would give utmost priority—and the mission was to extract the king from the dragon-kin's clutches. With a grim tightening of his jaw, the dragon opened his eyes and pumped his wings for greater speed toward the Blackwatch rendezvous point.

The pressure in his chest grew with every wing beat. How uncomfortable it was to hold the cold blast like this, but not knowing what he would confront when he reached the rendezvous point, he did not dare arrive unprepared. The distance whizzed by in mere moments, until Majestrin folded his wings to dive.

Five figures were on the run. Galdurith led a taller elf, clad in a long, opulent gold robe, much smudged and snagged. Anyone who had come with the detachment came garbed for battle, so logic implied this elf to be the king. Three more of the major's soldiers kept a frantic rearguard, the whites of their eyes visible even from a distance. As one, they looked up, and upon glancing down Majestrin's length, their expressions grew all the more incredulous.

A cacophony of chaos and crashing thundered from the woods that ringed the clearing where Majestrin found the reconnaissance team. Guttural shouts demanded blood for the elves' defiance of their edict. The dragon touched down in the clearing. Yes, they had gotten their king this far, but not without notice.

"Help His Majesty astride!" the major bellowed as he set his crossbow. He turned a vexed glare to the dragon. "Where is Vinyanel?"

"No time to concern yourself with that right now." The dragon stretched out his long neck and snatched King Saransaeloth in his mouth.

One of the Blackwatch soldiers uttered a strangled scream. Majestrin shot the soldier a weary look, then placed the king astride his back.

"Get him home!" Galdurith glared down the length of his crossbow. The bolt flew from his weapon, followed shortly by a yelp from somewhere within the obscured ranks of dragon-kin.

"One moment," Majestrin said. "No need to sacrifice the rest of you. Behind me, if you will."

The soldiers hesitated until the second time Galdurith ordered them to take the dragon's suggestion. Majestrin paused as the clatter in the woods to the east erupted into the clearing as well. A score of dragon-kin charged, brandishing serrated swords, claws, and maws full of ragged teeth.

Finally. From the constricted chamber in his chest, Majestrin heaved a great gust, and the detachment of dragon-kin that had barely cleared the underbrush faced the horror of an inescapable cloud of freezing death. The only dragon-kin soldier that survived was frozen on one side. To die as the others had would have been a greater mercy.

Galdurith stood, transfixed and blinking. Eventually, he turned and bowed to Majestrin. "Uh...well done. We thank you. Now if you would, His Majesty ought to get clear of any more trouble."

"I understand, Major. I have one more passenger to pick up, then we will be on our way to Delsinon."

"Ecleriast." Galdurith wrinkled his nose. He turned to his

soldiers. "Ryathos, regroup with the others and begin stage C. I will ensure His Majesty's safety in Ecleriast's absence."

The major hauled himself astride the dragon. Both the king's and Galdurith's legs trembled as they gripped Majestrin's sides. After this mission, he would need to adjust some individuals' expectations that he was like a mundane horse, to be lent like a beast in a livery stable.

For now, he only hoped Vinyanel had not gotten himself in so hot a stew that he and two terrified riders might struggle to intervene. Majestrin thrust his wings and sped back to the south.

16

CREO'S SIGHT

I WAVERED ON UNSTEADY LEGS, but forced an unruffled gaze to Scitherias. "So, the rumors of your influence are false, then. I have heard tell that you had progressed far beyond the lowly job of dispatching mere mortals. Are you not overdressed for this occasion?"

Scitherias smirked. "Nice try. I have not been goaded by either insults or flattery since before you were born, Captain. I shall remember your last words, however. They were amusing."

A string of language I did not understand, but that rang with an unwholesome timbre of obscenity, spilled from Scitherias' lips.

Jump aside.

I heard the command in my heart, and do not think I could have resisted the compulsion even if I had been so inclined. Just as I leapt to my left with more strength that I thought remained within me, the ground opened a ravenous maw beneath me. I clutched the loose earth with straining fingers, and was barely able to scrabble aside and avoid a plummet into bottomless depths.

I remembered the dagger on my belt, and threw it even as I

rolled away from the crumbling edge of the crevasse. To my profound shock, the blade actually sank into Scitherias's abdomen, and by the look upon his face, his disbelief matched my own.

With a stifled grunt, Scitherias pulled my dagger from his midsection and cast it aside.

Your shield.

Again, I failed to understand why I should want it, but just as I swung it in front of me, a sizzling bolt of red fire glanced off its battered surface and ricocheted away. The tree into which I deflected the bolt burst into a ruinous fireball that left nothing but a charred stump in its wake.

Scitherias growled in disgust. "I have other, more pressing matters on my agenda today, Ecleriast. Would you kindly die?"

This time, no warning came before my body launched across the glade and slammed into the flat leeward side of an immense boulder that thrust its stony head from the forest floor. Scitherias held a trembling hand out before him, his talons flexed into dreadful bands of scales and sinew. He paced slowly toward me. Dark, crushing, malevolent pressure enveloped my body, squeezing the very soul from within me. I gasped for breath but drew none.

"This might have been brief. Relatively painless, Captain. But now you have irked me, and so I choose to deal to you the most agonizing death the Darkness provides me." He flexed his fingers into a tighter clench, and I felt my every rib snap as one. My head throbbed as though my helm had shrunken around it to half its normal size. My vision swam. The pressure would not even allow me to cough. Was there something I was supposed to do?

Death stood close by; he held out the promise of an end to my suffering. But no, I dared not accept his invitation, however much of a relief it would be. Too much had I left undone on this mortal plane. The Chalice, back in enemy hands, wasting the valiance of too many good soldiers. My king? Saved, or throat gaping to spill his lifeblood on the indifferent soil? My homeland, now at risk of enemy discovery, infiltration, and attack. On top of all this, so many individuals had suffered wrongs at my temper or whim. Inexplicably, amidst my agony, my thoughts flitted to Veranna's tear-filled, amber eyes when I had lashed her with Creo's word. Perhaps the accusation had been true. But how wrong I had been to rebuke her as I would an inferior.

Scitherias squeezed again, and a loud pop from my pelvis wrenched me back to the present. The strength of all evil bore down upon me. Had it been an earthly weight, it would have driven me deep into the soil of this glade, flattened beyond recognition.

"Creo," I begged from my soul. "No power of mine can save me, and I confess it is my fault alone that I face this doom. If it be your will, rescue me from my folly."

He lifts all burdens that his servants will cast into his keeping. No weight is too great for the strength of the Almighty. No oppression can keep him from glorious flight.

Creo's words rang in my mind, not in a simple command, but in something far more potent. I knew the passage; it resided deep in my bones from repeated study. My lungs filled with air that I had not drawn for myself.

"Creo restrain you, servant of Darkness!" I choked out. I do not think Scitherias heard me, so stifled were my words by his crushing curse, but by the stricken expression on his face, I knew he felt the counter to his assault. The pressure lessened.

My voice grew in strength. *"Yea, though I am crushed under the lies of Darkness, though my enemies seek to cast me into the depths, even then shall I trumpet the faithfulness of the Almighty, Maker of all!"* Even though my joints wobbled, destabilized and out of alignment, I thrust my hands toward the draconic creature who had advanced within a dozen strides of me.

Scitherias scowled and took another step toward me.

I was not certain what I expected to happen, but my gesture's complete lack of effect deflated my momentary hope. I must have looked like a broken marionette. If only I had gleaned some fragment of understanding of Creo's Virtusen before I obviously needed one.

I had brought my lack of skill upon myself. I had squandered a matchless gift.

The flicker of concern that had licked across Scitherias's face evaporated. "You think you can frighten me away with a few words from a mere book of rhymes and impotent advice?" He clenched his outstretched talon again. I crumpled as my joints and tendons creaked and snapped.

"You are wrong, Scitherias..." The blackness that had lingered at the edges of my vision now closed on me. I saw everything through a small, dim window that shrank by the moment. Crushing cold enveloped me. Pain. Beyond despair. Beneath all this, however, a needling sensation crackled across my flesh. It fizzed from my skin like bubbles from the surface of sparkling wine.

The leaves on the ground around me stirred. The wild asters and the carpet of violets I had not noticed until now shuddered in a sudden breeze.

"Creo, the God of Creation, the One who tells the wind where it shall blow and upon whom it will spend its mighty wrath, spake *The Tree* unto his servants, and by its wisdom and its power, you shall face your doom!" Again, I did not know from whence the breath to speak the words came, even as I felt my lungs collapsing as if gripped in Scitherias's tightening claws, but out they tumbled. The prickle in my skin erupted, and I thought I would be flayed from within by the intensity.

The breeze in the wildflowers whipped into a gale that roared through the glade. Scitherias fell backward to the ground. His hold released upon me and I crashed from where he had pinned me to the rock. I huddled against the stone, seeking refuge from the fury of the swirling gusts. The maelstrom rose further, tearing through the glade and forcing Scitherias back. He clawed and scrabbled, but the tumult pushed on. The last thing I saw was the massive bole of an ancient sycamore, uprooted by the unearthly wind, plunging to the earth. Scitherias uttered one arrested scream, and then my world went black.

"Vinyanel, come back," a melodious voice said, the speaker shrouded in a veil of light that was bright, yet not glaring.

A gossamer touch lit upon my forearm, and nothing else. It was as though no part of my body had sensation except where that radiant hand and my flesh met. Again, the voice urged me, full of heartbreaking beauty. "Come to us, young Windrider."

My vision changed, not so much the opening of my eyes as a shifting of color and clarity. The radiance of the figure that summoned me faded, leaving behind Veranna's countenance, tense and furrowed.

I might have once recoiled at that revelation, but the luminous vision that lingered in my mind and soul, the voice filled with longing and a lifetime of pain, and made beautiful in its endurance, coaxed me to a change of heart. I believe I had, in that brief moment, seen Veranna as Creo saw her.

Then, all at once, the reality of my pain from the assault Lord Scitherias had perpetrated upon me crashed over me. I writhed on the ground.

Veranna placed a hand on my forehead. "Be still, Vinyanel. We will see to the lessening of your pain, but for now I am grateful you live."

My chest heaved as I fought for breath. "Veranna, can you forgive me? I cannot die without that assurance."

A small smile crept across the prophetess's face, but she said nothing.

"I have been careless. Flaunted yet squandered my gifts. Forgive my arrogance," I said in a broken whisper.

"It will be easier to forgive you now that you have offered me a few points upon which we can agree." Veranna's smile grew into a wry smirk. She pressed harder upon my forehead, summoning a legion of dancing colors to obscure my vision. My pain drifted away as the myriad hues enveloped me.

"By Creo's power, be healed, Captain. May he cleanse you from the shadow that sought your end," Veranna intoned.

And thus, the treetops, filtering green and gold sunlight through their interwoven boughs, grew clear to me again. The crunch of footfalls upon last year's fallen foliage came to my ears, and the pad of a heavy creature approached. I turned my head, expecting grogginess or vertigo, but to my shock, experienced nothing of the sort. I was tired, but it was the best sort of tired I had ever felt.

Majestrin smiled down at me.

"Do you plan on dashing to the brink of death every time we face a conflict, Captain?" he asked. "If so, I need to teach myself how to worry less as you lay prone, gray as ash and unbreathing."

"No, my friend," I said through a hearty laugh, a laugh like none I had uttered since the carefree days of childhood. "I have learned that no matter who insists, I am foolhardy to pursue trouble anywhere but upon your back. You are to become an extension of me. Something Veranna tried to tell me on the very day we met." I stood, brushing the debris from my mangled clothes and armor.

Some paces ahead of me, a tree with a bole as wide as my armspan lay upon the ground. From beneath it, Scitherias's scaly arm and clenched talon protruded. The earth beneath the trunk glistened with dark blood.

A hand clasped my shoulder from behind. I turned to look full in the face of High King Saransaeloth, his eyes fathomless and face beset with many concerns. I could have hugged him on sight, but I managed to maintain my composure.

"You have rid us of a formidable foe, Captain. I shall scribe the writ for your promotion as soon as we pass the fortress gates," His Majesty said.

"Begging your pardon, Your Majesty, t'wasn't I. This is Creo's work."

"Does he not work through his creation? Aye, I shall promote you, Captain, on one condition," the king said with a grin.

"Sir?"

"You listen to this half-elven tutor of yours and discover how to hear Creo's voice with better clarity." The king clapped me on the back. "No good leaving some to think of your victories as luck."

I looked back to the fallen tree. "Perish the thought, your Majesty." As my gaze lingered upon the place where Scitherias met his end, a glint that was not blood caught my eye. With slow, measured steps, I approached the gruesome place.

Upon closer examination, the gleam appeared to be a silver edge. Every eye focused upon me. I stooped, dug my fingers through the fouled mulch, and grasped the metal. Just as I suspected. I wrenched the thing free with a hard snap.

I held aloft a silver amulet that pictured a crossed sword and scroll—a talisman of passage into my home city. "Well, here is one," I said.

Galdurith moved to my side. "It is a start."

"What of the rest of the dragon-kin?" I said.

"Scattered," Saransaeloth replied. "Once Majestrin arrived, they broke into small squadrons and dispersed."

Leaving us no notion of which to follow for the blasted Chalice or the other talismans.

The king barked a single laugh. "Maker's mercy, Captain, the sun's scarcely risen and you've already done a good day's soldiering. I can practically hear the tempest of your thoughts."

"So much work remains—" I said.

"And not every dragon might be slain in a day, if you'll excuse the expression," the king said. "The time is coming, and swiftly."

"As swiftly as I can intercept it, by your leave," I replied. "Though I intend to gather more tools for the hunt." My eyes met Veranna's.

"Brace yourself, Captain," she said. "No test you have ever faced will compare to the tasks ahead."

"Not the least of which will be learning to stay awake during your lectures," I said. "I anticipate a great many of that sort of trial before I take on the others."

Veranna propped her hands on her hips, but the impish spark that flickered in her eye told me we had an understanding.

Majestrin fluttered, stirring our hair as we stood in the clearing. "Climb aboard, my friends."

I extended an arm to offer Veranna a leg up, but she shook her head. "When I can choose, Captain, I will take the grounded route."

I pulled myself into the black leather dragon saddle and ran my fingers over the stitching. It was a perfect fit, both for Majestrin and me, yet it remained strapped to the dragon only by his leave.

"Ready when you are, Majestrin," I said.

He stretched the pinions of his wings wide, the membranes between them filtering the morning sun like sheets of ice, and yet in that moment, my world brightened.

In a sinuous thrust, Majestrin propelled us skyward. I leaned into the wind. No doubt, the calling we would face together would be as vast as the heavens themselves.

DIVINE SUMMONS

THE WINDRIDER SAGA BOOK 1

REBECCA P. MINOR

To Vanessa! Thanks for finding us at the PA Ren Faire!

Rebecca Minor

REALM MAKERS

Third Edition, 2018

ISBN 978-0-9962718-1-3

Realm Makers Media

Pottstown, Pennsylvania

http://www.rebeccapminor.com

http://www.realmmakers.com

For Scott, Riley, Gabe, and Ben—
My would-be Windrider Battalion